MAIL-ORDER BRIDE MOMMY

MONTANA MAIL-ORDER BRIDES
BOOK ONE

LINDA FORD

MONTANA, 1890

Gwen Humber again scanned the train platform of Crow Crossing, Montana where she expected to be greeted by her future husband—a man she'd never met.

Four cowboys crossed the planks, their heels thudding on the wood. But none of them looked in her direction. Nor did they match the mental picture she had of Matthew Shannon. They'd exchanged three letters and in one he'd described himself as being of medium height, medium build with brown hair and brown eyes. On second thought, two of the four might have fit that description but they showed no interest in her presence.

"Miss Humber, Miss Humber."

Gwen turned toward the sound of her name. A trim, older woman in a navy dress and navy hat hurried toward her. Gwen's hand tightened on her satchel. Her breath caught in her throat. Had this woman been sent to inform her that Matthew Shannon wasn't coming? Had he already changed his mind and decided she wasn't a suitable candidate for his requirements? She no longer had a home back east. Everything she owned accompanied her. Her funds would allow her a few nights in a boarding house and then what?

Limited funds. No home. The lump in her throat settled into her heart as she admitted her predicament. She had no choice but to stay in the West. Pushing her shoulders back and pulling in a deep, steadying breath, she faced the future. Even if her prospective groom had changed his mind, she'd find a way to make a life for herself in this wild, beautiful country. Though her determination proved unable to suggest a solution.

"Miss Humber?" The breathless woman reached her side. "I'm Mrs. Ingram, friend to Mrs. Strong."

Gwen put on her best smile knowing it didn't reach her eyes. "Yes, I'm she." Mrs. Ingram was the preacher's wife whom Mrs. Strong worked with to help single young women find husbands in the west. No doubt she would offer assistance.

"Let's get you home." Mrs. Ingram signaled a porter and asked for Gwen's trunks to be delivered. "To the parsonage."

The parsonage? Further proof of her being rejected? She forced a breath into her struggling lungs and told herself to stay calm.

"Matt should have come himself, but he said he wished to have a chance to meet you in private." Mrs. Ingram fluttered her hand as if her announcement was of no significance. "Now come along."

A tiny doubt embedded in Gwen's thoughts. Perhaps she shouldn't have been so eager to accept this escape from her life back East. Three letters from him did not provide much information. He was a rancher with three brothers and he needed a wife. She dismissed her uncertainty as quickly as it came. He waited at the parsonage which indicated he still seemed interested in marrying her. She relaxed as she followed the older woman.

A dog raced in front of them, almost tripping her. She dodged a boy who tore after the dog, kicking up dirt in his wake. A pebble stung Gwen's face. She chuckled at the absurdity of her life at the moment. A mail-order-bride without a groom, in a strange town, following a woman she'd never met before.

Mrs. Ingram gave her a quizzical look. "You'll do just fine if you can find the humor in things."

"My mother would concur. In fact—" she lifted her hand dismissively, "never mind." No need to share one of her dearest memories with a stranger.

The skin around the older woman's eyes crinkled as she smiled. "It's perfectly acceptable if you don't tell

3

me everything. Matt's the one you should confide in. You two will have much to talk about."

Gwen readily agreed. Many times on the trip she'd imagined the two of them laughing together, revealing their deepest fears and dearest memories and finding sweet comfort as they learned about each other. Never mind that she'd agreed to a marriage in name only. Of course, for that to happen, she'd need to meet the man. She was about to ask when she could hope to do so when Mrs. Ingram stopped at a gate.

"This is us." A tidy house stood in a pretty yard. Two huge trees sheltered the front door and early flowers bloomed with the promise of more to come. Past the house was a white church with a bell in its steeple.

Gwen paused to admire it. "I love hearing church bells ring." She followed the woman into the house.

The preacher's wife stepped aside to reveal a man who rose at their entrance.

Even without Mrs. Ingram's introduction, she knew this was Matt Shannon. Her soon-to-be husband. Her heart rapped against her ribs like a trapped butterfly. She bit her bottom lip to still her reactions and took in a calming breath that failed its objective as her nerves continued to twitch.

Mrs. Ingram paused at the doorway. "You two need to discuss your plans." She exited the room, softly closing the door behind her.

"I'm pleased to meet you in person," he said, his

voice steady as if he experienced none of the tension she did. Maybe she'd sucked every bit of it from the room to her insides which continued to do strange flip-flops.

She focused so she could assess him. The way he'd described himself had led her to believe he was so ordinary she couldn't have picked him out in a crowd. To the contrary, she would have spotted his thick head of brown-like-chocolate hair across a room bursting with people. His brown eyes held her gaze in a steady look that caused her to think he was the sort of man she could count on. Relief sighed through her. "And I you."

"Am I as you expected?" he asked.

His uncertain question settled her last trembling nerve. "You're taller than you led me to believe."

A grin gave his face a friendly, kind look. "Guess I'm used to my brothers teasing me about being the shortest of the bunch."

"Am I as you expected?" She tried and failed to smile. She knew what she was. At twenty-three, considered an old maid by most. Plain according to many. Few saw how she tried to find the joy in everything, nor did they appreciate her loving ways. Except for her brother Maurice. Not that his appreciation had lasted.

"You're younger looking than I expected and not at all plain."

Heat rushed up her neck at his frank assessment.

But his words pleased her. Life with this man would not be unpleasant if he was always so generous in his comments.

"Where is the little girl I'm to take care of?" she asked.

"I left Lindy at the ranch. I thought it would be easier for us to take care of our business without her."

His response made sense, but the words sank to the bottom of Gwen's heart. She was anxious to meet four-year-old Lindy. Providing the child with a mother was the sole reason for their marriage. Gwen was satisfied the union would also provide her with a permanent home.

She swallowed down her disappointment before she answered. "I am agreeable to all your stipulations. A marriage in name only. A mother for Lindy. I'll run your house. By becoming Mrs. Shannon your home becomes mine. I believe that was all."

He rubbed his hands along his thighs.

Gwen sensed the movement signaled that he had something to say that she wouldn't like. The skin across her cheeks tightened as she waited for him to say what was on his mind.

"We know little about each other." He looked to her right as if unable to meet her gaze.

Her previous thoughts of sweet sharing threatened to fly away. "We can learn as we go along."

"I suppose we could." His eyes met hers, intense with—

The room was suddenly devoid of air. Her legs wobbled. She eyed the nearest chair but if she sat, he would tower over her. She stiffened her knees and waited.

He swallowed audibly. Which, her trembling heart warned, was not a good sign.

"It's important that I don't make a mistake." A brief pause as if considering his words. "That neither of us do. Lindy needs a mother but, in all fairness, I think we should be sure our agreement will be a good fit for her."

Agreement? Didn't he mean marriage? Her fingers hurt and she realized she had twisted them into a knot and forced herself to relax.

Matt rushed on as if needing to get his words out before she spoke. Not that she could think of a thing to say.

"You're a city girl and might find living on a ranch is not to your liking."

She shook her head. It didn't matter where she lived. Only that she could hope for it to be permanent. Now it looked unlikely. Her chin lifted. Her jaw muscles clenched.

Again, he hurried on. "I don't want Lindy to have another person snatched from her life. She needs stability. Structure. Permanence."

Gwen nodded. "I agree. It's also what I want." For herself as much as the child.

"Marriage is a serious, binding contract. I think

before we take that step, we should be certain it's what we both want. To make that possible, I suggest a one-month trial period." His eyes steady, he waited for her response.

"One month?" The words shot from her mouth with a heat she couldn't control. And then what? He'd send her on her way? She choked back disappointment. But she'd already decided she would stay in the West if he hadn't shown up. It wasn't what she wanted, nor what she'd planned. In her hopes and dreams, she'd envisioned a place where she could put down roots clear to bedrock. Roots so strong no one could ever rip her from her home.

He waited, a patient look on his face. Or was it stubborn? Determined? It was too early in their acquaintance to know for certain.

For a moment, she struggled to respond. Confusion and disappointment made thinking difficult. But she must state her opinion clearly. "It's not necessary on my part. I've already made up my mind." She smiled to ensure there was no sting or criticism in her words. "According to Mrs. Strong back home, Mrs. Ingram is an excellent judge of character and highly recommends you. That's enough for me." Besides this, she had no home to return to.

He no longer rubbed his hands up and down on his leg. Instead, he crossed his arms. "This is for Lindy's sake. I don't want her to be raised in a situation where there is arguing or anger."

Shock at such an idea left Gwen momentarily speechless. She gathered her wits and shook her head. "I'm not like that. My mother said I was—" She shrugged. "Never mind." She could remind herself of those words without blurting them out to everyone she crossed paths with. Though they hadn't sprung to her mouth when the dog raced across her feet. The mere idea made her chuckle.

Matt's eyebrows rose. "Is this something I should know? I believe if we are contemplating marriage there shouldn't be any secrets between us."

"Agreed." Now was not the time to keep her thoughts to herself unless they were hurtful. "It was something my mother often said to me. You see, I tend to find the humor in things. I perhaps laugh a little too often. You might find it trying." She paused, giving him a chance to say no but he didn't. "She called me her little ray of sunshine and I try to live up to her assessment."

"Do others find it bothersome?"

"No." She shrugged. "At least not that anyone's told me."

"Then let's assume it isn't. But perhaps you can see why I ask for a month of getting to know each other better."

He had a point. "Very well. A month." She would be on her best behavior and not do anything annoying. The idea that she would pretend to be other than what she was made her laugh.

He quirked one eyebrow. How did he do that?

She explained what had amused her. "You see what I mean? It's a perfect example."

He tipped his head in acknowledgment of her words. "Maybe we should do our best to be who we are."

Wheels rattled up the path and he gestured toward the sound. "I believe that's your luggage. I'll get it loaded and then we'll be on our way." He went to the adjoining room and spoke to Mrs. Ingram who waited for them to announce they were ready to proceed with their planned wedding. "We'll be leaving now."

Mrs. Ingram rushed up to them. "What about the ceremony? My husband is prepared to—"

"We've agreed to delay taking vows for a month." He was matter-of-fact in his announcement.

"But...but..." She sputtered. "You can't take her out to your ranch. With nothing there but men!" Shock made her voice squeak.

"And Lindy." Matt indicated Gwen should accompany him outside.

Her trunks, containing everything she owned, waited in the back of a wagon. She had her winter and summer clothing, two quilts her mother had put together, one she had made, a few other mementos from home, some books, and of course, her sewing notions.

Matt helped her to the seat. She smoothed her skirt and smiled. She was about to go to her new home and, trial period or not, she meant to prove she was ... she sought for a word to explain the deep yearnings of her heart. The only one she came up with was needed. But it was too weak. Maybe she meant necessary.

What she did know for certain was she intended to prove she was the best woman for the position Matt Shannon had offered.

MATT FLICKED the reins and headed the horses toward home. By rights, he should have brought the buggy and provided a proper ride for the woman who would become his wife if they still agreed after a month. But he'd had to pick up supplies and he'd had no idea how much luggage Miss Humber would have. As well, he should have picked her up at the train station, but he hadn't gone to that location since Corine had...well, since the last time he'd waited for her.

He slid a gaze to the woman at his side. She'd written that she'd been a housekeeper for her brother but was no longer needed now that the brother was getting married. She had helped care for children in several church families which gave him assurance she could handle Lindy. A plain-looking spinster was how she'd described herself. He'd imagined someone with eyes full of sadness and regret. He'd thought her mouth would be set in a permanent frown. Or at least be drawn back. She'd be a woman who had a rigid schedule, and regimented activities which were exactly what Lindy needed. The child had been running wild. Some discipline would put a stop to her mischief.

But Gwen was not at all like he'd expected. For one thing, she wasn't plain. She was... well, she wasn't plain. Her hair was brown but shone with brightness as if sunshine had burrowed along her scalp. Her brown eyes held a golden glint. She wasn't dour as he'd assumed she'd be. Even when she wasn't smiling her eyes twinkled and amusement seemed to hover on her lips.

No. She definitely wasn't what he'd expected.

Yes, she'd come highly recommended. And he was desperate. But was this what he wanted?

He gripped the reins so hard that his knuckles turned white, and he relaxed his fingers. At the same time, he admitted to himself he had no idea what he wanted. Apart from one thing. Lindy needed a home. A mother. Stability.

Before he and Gwen tied the knot, he had to be assured the child would be properly cared for. Lindy's parents, Merry and Roscoe, had allowed their daughter free run of the place. Roscoe was one of the ranch's top hired man and Matt's best friend. Merry cooked for them and ran the house. Since their passing, Lindy had grown undisciplined. It had to be stopped. This arrangement was solely for Lindy's benefit. He'd been clear that he wanted a marriage in name only. Matt had no need of love or emotional entanglements. In his experience, they simply made a man vulnerable to unsettled, painful feelings. He had only to look back as far as the accident that claimed Merry and Roscoe's lives. But if he cared to look further there was Corine.

Miss Humber had been recommended by the preacher's wife back in Illinois who facilitated introducing young women of marriageable age to young men out west who longed for a wife. In Matt's case, simply a mother for Lindy. They'd corresponded briefly. Three letters total. But there was some urgency to get things arranged for Lindy's sake. Neither his brothers nor their older cowhand had time to devote to the child.

Miss Humber—Gwen—had said she was eager to move forward with the wedding plans. According to the information Matt received, she was about to lose her home. It seemed they were both going to benefit from their decision. Thankfully, she'd agreed to a month's trial period. It sounded cold to say each needed to assess the other, but it was necessary in his mind. He didn't mean to make a mistake that would affect not only his life, but Lindy's. Parenting was still so new to him, he wasn't sure of his own path, much less how to tread with Gwen or he might have considered the one-month trial before Gwen started the trip. Instead, his decision had been formed on the trip to town. He regretted being so slow to see that a delay was wise.

"How is Lindy getting along?" Gwen asked. "I can't imagine how difficult it is for a four-year-old to lose her parents. Goodness knows it was hard enough for me when I was seventeen."

He glanced at the woman beside him and saw her lips tremble. Remembering her warning that she found life amusing, he was relieved to know not everything was humorous.

She continued. "And you lost your good friends at the same time." She briefly touched his sleeve. "I'm sorry."

He barely managed to keep from jerking away not needing or wanting that sort of behavior between them. "She's been doing remarkably well. Of course, she didn't have to leave her home so that helps."

"I'm sure it does." She opened her mouth as if she meant to say something more and he waited. "I expected you to meet me at the station." Her voice rose in a tentative question.

"I'm not comfortable waiting for a train." He inwardly sighed. No doubt she'd want to know why but he didn't like talking about his reasons. The painful past was best left untouched.

She shifted to watch him as she spoke. "I was afraid you didn't want anyone to see you greet me." A smile touched her lips though her eyes remained guarded.

When she didn't ask for his excuse for not being at

the train station, hands he didn't realize he squeezed so hard, relaxed. He shifted his thoughts to her comment. Did she think he'd be embarrassed that he'd ordered himself a bride? "I meant no personal slight. I don't care what opinion others have of my decision. I'm simply doing what I think is best."

She nodded. "Good to hear. Perhaps you could tell me about your brothers and your ranch?"

He settled back, glad to be talking of a safer subject. "First, the ranch isn't mine. It belongs to all the Shannons. I have a twin brother—Luke—"

She gave a burst of laughter. "There are two of you? You never mentioned that. Should make life interesting."

"I hate to quell your anticipation, but Luke is nothing like me." And that was an understatement.

"Whew. I'm relieved. Imagine the confusion if I couldn't tell you from him."

"You'll have no trouble." A strange twinge of jealousy—both unfamiliar and unwelcome—touched his nerves at understanding she would no doubt compare the two of them. Perhaps she'd find Luke and his ready sense of humor more to her liking. Matt had more than once been told he took life too seriously. Shoving the thought away, he continued. "We have an older brother, Riley. He's twenty-six. And a younger brother, Andy, who is twenty-two. Luke and I are right in the middle at twenty-four."

"What are they like?"

His brothers? He studied his answer. "Riley is serious. Andy is…well, being youngest, he is still adventurous." He didn't know how else to describe his youngest brother.

"What about Luke?"

"He's the sort who thinks things can wait until tomorrow." Matt congratulated himself on keeping rancor from his tone, but he and his twin had often bashed heads over that attitude.

"If he's the opposite of you then you're the sort who likes to get things done right away?" she asked.

"I didn't say the opposite but yes, that about describes us I suppose."

She considered this information for a moment before she spoke again. "Didn't you say you had your own house?"

"We all do, though Andy lives in the big house Pa built. Guess we've all been spending a lot of time there lately. Since the accident that left a little girl without parents."

"Where is Lindy in all of this?"

That was often the question. Where was Lindy? "We've taken turns staying with her. Including Wally." But they had a ranch to run and couldn't keep chasing after a little gal who liked to run off when the mood hit.

"Wally?"

"He's our oldest hired man." By rights, he should have provided this information in one of his letters.

Instead, they'd mostly contained his plans for Lindy, and of course, facts about the child. The last missive had contained directions on getting to Crow Crossing. "Sometimes, he's our cook. Lindy's parents, Roscoe and Merry, moved in to run the house when Pa was alive and stayed on afterward. Merry cooked for us. Roscoe was a cowhand." He sucked in a breath and rushed on before Gwen could ask any more questions. He didn't want to talk about the pain he felt over losing his best friend and the man's wife. "I don't know if I was clear about what I want for Lindy. She needs firm guidance. You'll need to establish rules and a routine right from the start. She'll balk, of course, but like a filly being broken to ride, she'll soon settle down and appreciate it."

"A filly being broken?" Gwen sputtered with laughter. "She's a four-year-old child, not a horse." Amusement fled from her eyes, and she gave Matt a defiant look. "I most certainly will not be treating her like one."

She was already defying him? A city girl who knew nothing about ranch life? How was he to keep Lindy safe if this woman, meant to take care of her, ignored his warnings? Good thing he'd asked for a trial period. He reined in the horses, allowing the wagon to stop, and faced Gwen full on. "Are you telling me you won't follow my orders? I find that unacceptable."

She held his gaze a moment then lowered her head to study her hands as they twisted into a hard knot.

"I'm sorry. I spoke out of turn. I am usually very compliant." She sucked in air like a hard-run horse. "But am I not to be allowed to make decisions according to what I think best?"

"Well, certainly you are. I won't interfere with the meals or the housework but when it comes to Lindy—"

She lifted her head and tilted her chin, her eyes shone with a boldness he'd not expected. "You might as well take me back to town at once."

---

2

*H*e'd let her run the house, but he meant to dictate how she was to mother little Lindy? The child was to be raised like he'd raise a horse? The very idea of doing so made her want to jump off the wagon and walk back to town. She shifted to the side, prepared to alight. Let him bring her luggage back without her company.

He caught her elbow. "Hang on. Let's work this out. Lindy requires someone immediately."

And Gwen needed a home although, perhaps she could throw herself at the mercy of Mrs. Ingram until she could arrange something else.

She sank back. "There is nothing you can say that will convince me she needs to be treated like a horse."

He scrubbed at his chin. "I didn't mean to suggest she should. I was simply using that as a… a…"

"Exactly. There's no way to excuse such a comparison."

He leaned back as if her protests meant nothing to him. As if her words were annoying insects.

He interrupted her thoughts. "I don't believe that's the real problem." His eyes demanded her attention. "You haven't even reached the ranch and you're already prepared to defy me."

She lowered her gaze. What had come over her? She'd never been defiant in her life. Yes, and where had that gotten her? She drew in enough air to fill the wagon and still felt like she'd forgotten to breathe. "I'm sorry. It's only that I don't care to have people compared to animals or inanimate objects. It's insulting." Her brother, Maurice, was now married to the woman who had used many of them in her description of Gwen. A suffocating vine. A leech. A clingy cat. That one really hurt as Patricia had been eyeing Gwen's pet cat when she uttered those words. Gwen couldn't leave the room without the feline following her, meowing if Gwen was out of sight. "I'm not like a cat." Whoops, she hadn't meant to blurt that out.

He quirked one eyebrow. "A cat? Why would you say that?"

She shifted her gaze to the rolling plains behind him. "It was just an example." She smiled as she spoke though she felt no humor. There was no need for him to know every detail of her life.

He waited.

"Fine, it was something my sister-in-law said. She compared me in an unflattering way to our pet cat."

He pursed his lips as he considered her answer then shook his head. "I can't imagine what she could say that was offensive. Cats have claws. Are you saying you're quick to scratch people? Was your objection to being asked to establish discipline and routine for Lindy an example?" He sounded wary. And rightfully so when he put it that way.

"Our cat was needy. She cried if I left the room. Patricia said I was like that. Not willing to let my brother go."

"I see."

How could he possibly know how much that assessment had hurt?

"Did you scratch her eyes out?" The skin around his eyes crinkled and his lips curved in a quick smile.

Did he mean to be amusing or was he wary of how she would act? But the idea of turning her claws against Patricia made her laugh. "It never crossed my mind. Nope, I left and that's why I'm here."

"I'm sorry she said such things to you. And I'm sorry for comparing Lindy to a horse. Now if that's settled, shall we continue?"

"One more thing."

This time both eyebrows rose.

"Am I going to need your approval for everything I do with Lindy?" She meant to do her best to please the man, but she couldn't consult with him about every decision.

"No, of course not. But she does need rules and structure." She could almost hear his teeth creak as his jaw muscles twitched. "Are you opposed to that?" He had not started the wagon rolling again and Gwen knew her answer would dictate which direction it would go—either onward to the ranch or back to town. She considered her words carefully knowing that her future hung on what she said.

"My belief is that the most important thing I can give her is affection and attention. My hope is that my work will never keep me from time spent with her. I want her to enjoy life." She held his dark eyes in a steady gaze. "I want her to appreciate every joy the world offers." She lowered her eyes to her hands clutched in her lap. What she said next might be inappropriate and unwelcome, but she must say it. "If I can help you do the same it would please me." Her breath caught part way up her throat as she waited for his response.

He grunted. "Your concern on my behalf is unneeded. I have everything I want in life—the ranch, my brothers, and Lindy. Save your energy for other things."

Very well. But his resistance wouldn't change how she meant to live her life. "But you don't mind if that's how I deal with Lindy?"

"Gwen, all I ask is that Lindy is safe, obedient, and happy."

Her trapped air released in a noisy gust. "Well, I certainly don't object to that."

"Good. Now let's get going. I'm sure you're anxious to see your new home."

Relief warmed her veins now that they'd resolved their first challenge. "Indeed, I am." Home. It was such a welcoming word.

"I suppose you've noticed the mountains."

Amusement that he should think he needed to point them out tugged her mouth into a grin. "I could hardly miss them. They're majestic. Don't they make you want to cry hallelujah?" She hugged herself as she studied the blue peaks. "You can almost hear them shout for joy to God." Her eyes stung with happy tears at the way they made her feel. She brought her gaze to Matt. His eyes rounded with what she hoped was surprise and perhaps even, approval. Pleased at making him look at her that way, she chuckled. "Like I said, I mean to enjoy life. I trust you aren't put off by my words."

He blinked and shook his head. "No. It reminds me of something."

"Really? Something good, I hope." She waited for him to explain. Like Mrs. Ingram said and as they'd agreed, they needed to share their thoughts and memories.

"Sounds like something my ma would have said but I can't remember exactly."

Was he telling the truth or avoiding an honest answer? She didn't know. But if they were to get to know each other, they must talk. She prepared to be the first one to start but before she could do so, he pointed down the roadway.

"There's your first glimpse of the place." The deep timbre of his voice suggested satisfaction, pride, or both. He stopped the wagon.

Eager to see her new home, she leaned forward to study the scene. A row of buildings stood on a ridge overlooking a narrow valley. Some were obviously houses, one larger than the others. She made out barns and other structures.

"It's like a little town." A welcoming little town. Sweetness coated her tongue. Warmth pooled in her stomach. Her hands lay loose in her lap. This was to be her new home. Her forever home if he married her.

He chuckled. "Maybe so. Before us is Shannon Valley. All the houses overlook it."

The green valley, the purple-blue mountains, and the sun-bright sky filled her heart with joy. "You must have a wonderful view."

"We do."

Before he picked up the reins again, she turned toward him. "Matt, I told you that I was losing my home." Their letters had been few in number and brief. Basically, they had both expressed the desire for marriage and laid out the terms to which they could agree. But neither of them had said much else. She reasoned there would be lots of time to learn those things afterward.

"You said your brother was getting married," he said.

Her nod was short and quick. It still hurt to acknowledge how easily she'd been replaced. "I've been his housekeeper since our parents died. We lost our home at that time." She'd never forget the helpless feeling of being without a roof over their head. The mere memory sent a shiver down her arms. "Pa worked for one of the shipping companies operating boats on the Mississippi. The house we lived in belonged to them. Suddenly, we were homeless. It was a hard time for both of us. We held each other up through it." At her urging, her brother had asked for a position with the same company their father had worked for. She'd arranged to rent a place to live, selling a piece of her mother's jewelry to pay for the first month. "Maurice got a job with the same company, and we found a small house."

She fixed her gaze on the mountains. *God of the mountains, You are my strength.* "It was a good arrangement, but I suppose I was foolish to think it would last forever. Maurice met Patricia. Although he said I would always have a home with them, she had other ideas. And wasn't terribly subtle about them. She said I was a leech, clinging to my brother." She would not mention the other things Patricia had said in her desire to persuade Gwen to leave.

She continued, hoping he wouldn't detect the slight tremor in her voice as she recalled those painful days. "My friend told me Mrs. Strong arranged several marriages to men in the west and I appealed to her." It was comforting to know she had a place to go even if it was to strangers. "I stayed until the wedding then started my journey here."

"I'd say your brother's loss is my gain." Kindness warmed his eyes.

"Thank you," she whispered. "Mrs. Strong said I should think of it as God's timing."

"Do you?"

"I try." She gave a brisk nod. "I'm grateful that I have a new home." And she'd do her absolute best to pass the one-month trial period. She did not care for the unsettled feeling of having no place to belong.

As MATT GUIDED the wagon onward, across the valley and up the slope to where the trail branched off toward the Shannon place, he again thought how Gwen was not what he expected. Only this time, he didn't mean her looks so much as her attitude. She'd reacted strongly to being told how to raise Lindy. He gave the idea a moment of reflection. Was it simply that he'd suggested the child's needs were similar to those of a horse? A grin tugged at his mouth. That was an unfortunate comparison.

Then she'd told him bluntly and without rancor about how her sister-in-law had treated her. It seemed to him that she was wise to get as far away from that woman as possible.

A small figure raced toward them, mouse-colored hair flying behind her, skirts billowing out, her arms spread wide.

Matt chuckled as he stopped the wagon. "You are about to meet Lindy."

Gwen leaned forward and laughed. "She looks like a bird about to take flight."

"I believe she would fly if it was possible." Amusement rounded his words.

Lindy reached them. Matt held out a hand and pulled her up. She breathed hard, warmth emanating from her. "Hi, Uncle Matt." Her gaze was on Gwen. Assessing, measuring.

Matt hoped she liked what she saw. The child could be troublesome if she decided against something. "Lindy, this is the woman I told you about. Miss Humber."

Silence hung between them like heated air, waiting for a breeze to drive it away.

Gwen broke the quiet. "I'm pleased to meet you, Lindy, and you may call me Aunt Gwen, if you like." She chuckled. "You ran so fast, you were almost flying."

Lindy nodded, her expression serious. "I run really, really fast." She slid a glance at Matt and away again. "Sometimes I run so fast Uncle Matt can't catch me."

"I see." Gwen nodded solemnly as her gaze met Matt's.

Maybe now she was getting an understanding that this child needed some rules and discipline.

"Everyone is waiting to meet you." Lindy studied Gwen with narrowed eyes. "Uncle Luke said you and Uncle Matt were getting married."

"We decided to wait a little while." She spoke gently, calmly to the child which met Matt's approval.

Lindy cocked her head. "Why?"

Gwen looked to Matt as if expecting he would answer but he wanted to hear what she would say. Acknowledgment flickered through her eyes. "He needs time to decide if we suit each other."

"Suit? What's that mean?"

"It means there are some things you shouldn't rush into."

"Would you like to fly?"

Lindy's question startled Matt. Not that he wasn't unfamiliar with her swift changes of topics.

Gwen laughed. "It does look exciting but only if I had wings. Being on the ground watching the birds swoop and soar is fun too."

"Like this." Lindy held her arms out and flapped like a bird.

Gwen met Matt's gaze. Her eyes were sparkling.

Her mouth curving. She was obviously amused by the child. Her smile flattened and the moment hung from a fragile thread as a silent message passed between them. Had she realized that he was, at that very moment, assessing her?

"Sit down, Lindy, so we can continue," he said.

She perched on the edge of the seat between Matt and Gwen and continued to wave her arms as if by doing so, she powered the wagon forward. Suddenly, she stopped.

"Uncle Luke said I hafta move to your house."

"That's right. Remember we set up a bed in one of the bedrooms."

"What if I don't want to?"

He didn't point out that things would be different now. Before he answered, Gwen spoke.

"I'm hoping we can do many fun things together."

Lindy bounced around to look at her. "Like what?"

"Tell me what you like to do."

"Fly." She again waved her arms like a bird.

Gwen chuckled. "Anything else?"

Lindy sat back. "Mama used to read to me. I liked that. And Papa chased me." She shifted her gaze to Matt. "You 'member?"

"Of course, I do." He'd chased her too, but he understood it wasn't the same as Roscoe being there to do it. Even though he couldn't replace her father, he'd do his utmost to give the child a happy, secure home.

Gwen spoke. "Maybe you'll like the book I brought you. Do you like games and picnics?"

Lindy lowered her arms and nodded.

They turned the last corner toward the houses.

"Ma and Pa and us boys lived in that cabin to begin with." Matt pointed out the original cabin and then directed her attention to the house further along the trail. "The big house Pa built." They approached the building. "It's where Luke lives."

"And you and everybody." Lindy squinted at Matt as if she thought he needed reminding of that fact.

It was true, since Roscoe and Merry's accident, they'd congregated there, mostly to take care of Lindy.

"And me. I live there." Lindy sat back hard enough to make the seat bounce. "Now maybe I don't."

"But what fun we'll have," Gwen said.

"Good." The child appeared satisfied with the promise.

It was on the tip of Matt's tongue to remind them both that there were also rules and schedules but a warning look from Gwen made him change his mind.

Instead, he returned to telling her about the place. Before he could continue, Lindy spoke.

"That's Uncle Wally's house." Lindy pointed to the original home. "'Cept he's been at Uncle Luke's house to help cook and look after me."

Before her death, Merry had cooked for them. Her absence left a hole that a cook couldn't replace but it would be nice to have someone to take care of proper meals for the child.

"Uncle Matt, who's gonna do it now?"

"Aunt Gwen will cook for us, and Uncle Wally and the others will take turns just like they have been." Unless Riley retreated to his own house and batched. Luke, too, might prefer his own company which would leave Andy on his own though Wally still felt the need to take care of the youngest Shannon from time to time.

Lindy studied Gwen as if by doing so she could assess what sort of changes her presence meant.

Matt went on with his description of the place. "Next to the big house is Riley's. Further along, is mine." It lay tucked in behind trees providing a bit of privacy. "Luke's is the one sitting on the piece of land that juts out."

"What made you all build your own houses if none of you are married?"

"Pa's wishes. He thought we should all have our own homes." He also thought each of them should wed and raise a family. Lots of little Shannon children. So far, they'd only achieved the houses and they all seemed content with that.

Luke strode out of the big house and stood waiting to greet them. In a more sedate fashion, the others followed—three men flanking him—Riley, Andy, and Wally. Great. Why not overwhelm Gwen at first glance?

He prepared to apologize but his words died on his lips as she chuckled.

"Looks like I'm attracting a lot of attention." Humor flashed in her eyes like the sun on running water. "I'm not used to that."

He was at a loss to know what to say. She was bound to be the center of interest around here. Would she object to it? He wondered what she saw. A crew of men. All bareheaded at the moment. Riley, tall and thin. Dark brown hair and even darker eyes. Eyes that seemed to hide things. Luke, Matt's twin, taller than Matt, with lighter hair and lighter eyes. Then there was Andy. He was more like Ma than any of them with blond hair and blue eyes. He was also the tallest of them by one inch. And Matt knew that because, for years, Andy insisted on everyone measuring against the door frame.

Wally was older though Matt had no idea how old the man was. His hair was black with streaks of gray. His eyes were dark though Matt couldn't have told Gwen what color. It wasn't something that concerned him. The fact that Wally was a good man was of more importance than his eyes. He'd been faithful to the Shannon family for years.

The wagon stopped. Luke stepped forward and held out his arms to catch Lindy as she jumped down. He set her on the ground to let her continue pretending to fly.

Matt helped Gwen to the ground and then turned to introduce her to the waiting men.

Not waiting for Matt to make the first move, Luke stepped forward and took her hand. "Let me welcome you as my sister-in-law."

Lindy paused from flapping her arms. "They never got married."

Four pairs of eyes bored into Matt.

"Why not?" Riley demanded.

Matt's reasons were sound, but he wasn't sure he could explain them satisfactorily.

Luke chuckled, saving Matt the need to get his thoughts sorted out. "Maybe she'd prefer the other twin. The better one."

Matt sighed heavily at the way Luke brushed his hair back off his forehead. He always did think he was the better-looking of the pair and maybe he was right.

Before Gwen said anything, Matt answered the questions hovering in the air. "It's a temporary delay while we make sure of what we both want." Thankfully, Gwen didn't repeat what she'd said to him. That she was ready to proceed without a trial period.

Luke leaned back on his heels. "Sure seems like you're asking for her to pick between us."

Andy leaned over the side of the wagon. "Did you get the peaches?"

"A case of them." Matt turned to explain to Gwen. "That's Andy's favorite treat but I'm sure he'll share them with you."

"Sure." Andy waved a hand without looking at them as he eyed the supplies. Not until he'd located the box of tinned peaches did he step back.

"You take the gal to your house and get her things inside then come back here." Wally wagged a finger at Matt and jabbed it at the others. "I made a meal for us. Didn't figger the little lady would want to start cooking right off."

Matt helped Gwen back to the wagon seat and drove along the trail connecting the houses. His brothers and Lindy trotted after him.

Minutes later, Gwen's luggage had been carried in. The supplies for his house were on the table and his brothers had taken the wagon to unload the goods for the big house. Lindy raced through the rooms, still flapping like a bird.

Gwen followed Lindy more slowly, going from room to room. Matt crossed his arms and waited for her to say something. Did the house meet her approval? He realized he'd said little about it but then three letters didn't give him room to go into minor details. Instead, he concentrated on the important things. Why he wished for a mail-order bride and what he expected from one.

His fingers twitched on his arms. What if she didn't like the house? Would it be the reason for her to refuse to marry him? She frowned slightly as she went to the next room. That didn't seem like a good sign.

3

Gwen went from one room to the next, Lindy trailing after her.

The first held a bed with a green blanket on it. The tousled appearance made her think this was where Matt had slept though she got the impression the men were spending their nights at the bigger house for Lindy's sake. A wardrobe stood in one corner.

She moved to the second bedroom, the bed neatly made with a multi-colored quilt on top. A chest of drawers sat next to the bed. It looked ideal for a young girl.

The double bed in the last room had a white crocheted coverlet. She turned to speak to Matt. "Did your mother make that?"

He nodded, his gaze lingering on the bed. "She did."

"It's to be my room?" Or the bridal suite depending on when he'd decided to delay the wedding.

He nodded. "It was supposed to be for us." His voice thickened then he glanced away, giving a slight shrug of one shoulder.

Did his answer mean he'd had second thoughts late in the game, perhaps on his way to town? Although he'd explained his reasons, she still felt...well, something more than disappointment. Almost like she had been weighed and found wanting even before he saw her. But she'd agreed to his terms.

She returned to the generous-sized living room where Matt stood waiting, his arms at his waist as if he was nervous. Lindy remained in the room that was to be hers.

"The place looks nice," Gwen told Matt.

"Pa insisted each of the houses must have three bedrooms. One for the parents, one for boys, and one for girls. He expected there to be lots of little Shannons."

Heat stung her cheeks. According to their agreement, there would be no little Shannons in this house. Even Lindy had a different last name. She guessed he'd been hurt by a woman. That would explain his insistence on a marriage in name only. Not unlike her own reasons. Her previous beaus had made it clear that Gwen had nothing to offer a handsome young man. Here, in this house, she could find permanency and value by mothering Lindy and being a good housewife.

"Where do you want your trunks?" He glanced down at her luggage.

His question brought her to her present situation. By way of answer, she grabbed the handle on one side of the first chest. He took the other and they carried it to the bedroom and parked it against the wall then returned for the second and put it at the foot of the bed. She unlocked them both but would take care of the contents later.

Matt left the room and as soon as she finished with the locks she followed him, circling the living area, aware of Matt watching and waiting. Maybe as uncertain of the next step as she was.

Directing her attention to the room itself, and away from questions about the future, she touched the back of the sturdy-looking settee in chestnut brown fabric. Expecting it to be harsh under her fingers she was surprised to discover it soft. "Is this leather?"

"Yes. Pa had the hide tanned by one of his native friends."

"It's nice." She moved on. There was a wooden rocking chair and two ladder-backed chairs beside a table with a lamp on top. A lacy doily and a little knickknack or a book would make the table less utilitarian. A tall bookcase stood against one wall holding half a dozen titles. She didn't stop to read the spines but moved on to the window and gasped.

"The view is spectacular." She looked over Shannon Valley, the colors fading from the bright green grass, and the vivid pink and purple of wild-flowers in the foreground to muted shades on the other side of the valley. And beyond that, the rugged Rockies in variegated blues with white tops like care-lessly iced cakes. "I could never grow tired of seeing this." Her heart swelled with emotion.

"Another of Pa's decrees. We had to build the houses to allow us to see the mountains."

She slowly tore herself from the window. "Your pa sounds like a very wise man."

"Yup."

She chuckled at the way he spoke, his pride obvious then she took in the rest of the room with a glance. So much potential. Through the doorway to the left, she entered the kitchen and dining area. A table to one side had six chairs circling it. Supplies covered its surface. The kitchen held a worktable, a shiny black-and-chrome stove, and lots of cupboards. Two doors exited to the right. The first revealed a large pantry and storage area. The shelves held an array of baking pans, jars, and crocks. The other door led to a cloak room with many hooks and shelves. Only one coat and a winter hat hung there. She opened the back door on the far side of the little room and looked out on trees and bushes sheltering them to the east and north. Luke's house sat further along the trail.

There was so much to explore, and she meant to do so once she'd settled in. She returned to Matt, waiting by the table.

"Well, what do you think?" he asked.

She clasped her hands at her waist, a gesture that hid the bubbling joy of her new home. "It's more than I expected."

"Really? What did you expect?"

"I read about the tarpaper shacks many bachelors live in." A crude frame shelter wrapped inside with black tar paper to provide a degree of protection. She almost laughed aloud at her assumption.

"And yet you came?" He shook his head.

"I figured I could improve things." Her gaze went around the room. "But this won't be the challenge I imagined." She turned full circle. "I can't wait to start."

"I'll help put supplies away. Just tell me where you want them."

She grabbed a box and carried it to the pantry. He followed with a crate. She began to unload items.

He observed for a moment. "What's your system?"

Her hands stopped in midair. "System? For what?"

"How you organize the supplies." He made it sound like she should understand what he meant.

"I put things on the shelves and find them when I need them."

He took the items she'd unloaded, and moved them to one side, sorting them into neat rows. Were they set in place alphabetically, by size, or by use? He then took the canned goods from his box and arranged them neatly on another shelf. She could tell those were sorted so the beans were all together, the peaches in their own row, and everything lined up like soldiers.

She watched as he emptied the entire crate then stood back brushing his hands together in satisfaction.

"There. At a glance, you can see exactly what you have on hand."

She slowly resumed taking items from her box and shelving them, trying to decide how she felt about having him choose the way she should do it. A little imp made her want to scatter the cans into disarray. But that would be childish.

He returned with another crate.

Only one thing concerned her. "Are you going to check on this and make sure I do it according to your standards?"

He stopped taking items from the box and stepped back. "I was only trying to be helpful."

They studied each other. She tried to find humor in the strain between them. And failed. She managed a smile, but it felt forced.

His eyes were wary. Was he seeing her as difficult? Challenging every suggestion he made, though to be fair, his *suggestion* about how she was to care for Lindy had sounded more like an order.

Then it hit her. They were acting like opponents. She didn't want to fight. "If that's what you expect then I will do it." She took items from the box and arranged them in what she hoped was a logical way.

He stood back for several minutes then lifted a sack of cornmeal and another of rice and placed them on a lower shelf. The air between them was stiff with uncertainty.

How was she to erase that feeling? And make it clear she didn't plan to question every bit of advice he gave?

Before she could frame a proper statement, a crash resounded through the house. Matt dropped the box and dashed in the direction of the noise, Gwen right behind him.

LINDY. Was she in trouble or causing trouble? The noise had come from the bedroom where Gwen's belongings had been taken and Matt didn't slow his steps until he was inside the room. The source of the sound was obvious. Books lay scattered across the floor.

The child responsible for the mess was missing.

Gwen rushed past him. "My things." She gathered items up, piled them on the floor by the trunk then sat beside the stack. Her gaze scanned the room and came to a stop at her right. She lifted a finger to Matt and directed his gaze to a pair of feet barely visible under the bed.

"Lindy, come out." His voice revealed his anger at her misbehavior.

The pair of feet withdrew further.

Gwen rose and touched his arm. "Let me try." She spoke so softly Lindy wouldn't hear.

He thought of arguing. Pointing out that the child should be disciplined but perhaps this was a chance for him to evaluate how Gwen would deal with Lindy's trying behavior. He nodded consent.

She turned toward the bed. "Lindy, it's all right. No harm done. I'm guessing you were looking for the book I promised you. Come here and I'll get it for you."

Inch by inch the feet emerged, followed by the rest of Lindy. She looked defiant, knowing she deserved a scolding at the very least.

Gwen reached into the trunk and brought out a book. Something about a child searching for a star. Matt couldn't imagine what sort of story that would be, but Lindy took it eagerly.

"Thank you. I'm sorry." She tipped her head toward the pile of books.

"You're forgiven but, in the future, I'd like you to ask before you touch things in my room. Understood?"

Matt leaned forward and perhaps sensing that he might want more than an apology from her, Lindy darted away. He sank back on his heels. He'd agreed to let Gwen manage it and she had. No tears. No protests. So why was he out of sorts?

Gwen considered him. "Did I do something wrong?"

He shrugged. "You dealt with it differently than I would." He scrubbed his hand over his head. Then it hit him. That was how Merry would have spoken to the child. He strode from the room and stopped at the window, his gaze on the distant mountains but his thoughts filled with memories of Roscoe and Merry. "Roscoe worked for us before he met Merry. Guess he was about my best friend in the whole world."

Gwen came to his side. Not saying anything. Just standing beside him gazing at the same thing.

"He met Merry when he went to Fort Benton one winter. He returned in the spring with her as his bride. Ma had been dead a couple of years and we welcomed her to run the house." He drew in a deep breath. "The girl must have wondered what she'd gotten herself into. But she managed really well. She learned to be a good cook." He paused as memories washed over him. He chuckled. "The first time she made a big batch of bread she must have mismeasured something. The loaves sank in the middle." He shifted to look at Gwen while he spoke. "How we teased her about that. Well, mostly it was Luke who did the teasing." Matt had warned Luke to stop a couple of times. But Luke had laughed at his concern.

Matt continued. "And then little Lindy was born.

She got a lot of attention. I worried she might get spoiled but Merry insisted a child couldn't know too much love." He heaved a huge sigh. "Guess I need to remember that. It's been hard on her. Losing her parents. Having only busy men to care for her. I'm grateful you're here to fill in that gap."

Gwen's smile caught the light of the sun. "I'm glad I'm here too."

Lindy ran past the window, both arms out like wings, the pages of the book Gwen had given her flapping in the wind.

"I should tell her to put the book in her room." Matt took a step toward the door.

Gwen caught his arm. "I gave it to her. Besides, she isn't hurting it."

He stopped, looked at her hand resting on his sleeve, and swallowed hard. "Very well."

"Thank you." She stepped back, ducking her head. Then she looked up and smiled. "I think if we bear in mind that we both want what is best for the child, we'll manage just fine."

He had no argument against that and nodded. "Couldn't ask for more."

Lindy raced in the back door letting it bang shut in her wake. She skidded into her room and returned without the book. "I'm hungry. Uncle Wally is gonna feed us."

"Then let's go eat." Matt waited for Gwen to fall in step with him as Lindy ran ahead through the thicket of trees that sheltered his house and yard. They reached Riley's house. Gwen slowed her steps to study it. "It looks a lot like yours."

"Riley insists he wasn't interested in marriage but built the house to please Pa. But he lives like one of your tarpaper bachelors."

She stopped walking. "That is not a tarpaper shack."

"Might as well be. All he cares about is a warm plate of stew, coffee that would burn your insides out, and a place to sleep. Merry used to go over there and get the bedding every so often to wash it. Roscoe always teased her because she wore his gumboots to clean the place."

Gwen's face broke into a wide smile that erupted into an amused grin. "You paint a delightful picture."

He chuckled. "Ma would roll over in her grave to know how he lives."

"Is he going to be at supper?" Her eyes sparkled.

"I expect so. He doesn't mind others cooking for him."

"This ought to be interesting."

Interesting? What did she mean? As they resumed their journey Matt wondered if he'd done the wrong thing to reveal so much about his older brother. But he couldn't take back his words, and they reached the big house without him warning her to be cautious of what she said.

All his brothers were there waiting. Wally was at

the stove. "It's about ready," the older man announced as he pulled a roasting pan from the oven.

Matt guided Gwen to the far side of the table and held the chair for her. Lindy sat between them as Wally placed loaded platters and full serving bowls in the middle of the table.

Matt looked around the table taking in all the changes. No doubt the others were noting the same thing. Ma had been gone for some time, Pa just a year ago, Merry and Roscoe a short time ago, and now a newcomer in their midst.

"This is different," Andy commented.

"But nice." Luke nodded his approval.

"Mama used to sit there." Lindy pointed to Wally. "Papa sat there." She pointed to the spot across the corner. "Said it was so's he could help."

Silence followed her words.

Gwen shifted her gaze to Matt, but he didn't know what to say. She waited a moment then turned back to Lindy. "I'm glad you told me."

Lindy nodded then with the quick changes she often exhibited said, "I'm hungry."

"I'll say grace." Riley cleared his throat and then murmured a short prayer.

Matt couldn't help but think of words his pa had spoken over each meal. *We are blessed beyond reason. Never lose sight of that.* They seemed appropriate today with someone here to help with Lindy.

They passed around the food, everyone loading

their plate. Except for Lindy who chose only her favorites—potatoes and gravy, but no roast beef. Peas but no turnips. No one said anything about what she ate. He'd need to tell Gwen that Lindy had refused food for so many days after her parents' deaths that he was happy to see her eat anything at all.

Riley turned to Gwen. "How was the trip?"

"Long." She chuckled. "I met some interesting people and saw some beautiful country."

"What kind of people do you consider interesting?" Andy asked.

"Most people are, I suppose."

Matt thought that might about sum up what he'd observed about Gwen's personality. People and life, itself, appeared to be fascinating to her.

"For instance," she continued. "There was this older man. Gray hair, gray whiskers, reedy voice. He told me he was once a gunfighter. Then he held up his hand. Now he shakes too much." She chuckled. Her eyes flashed with amusement. "There was a younger man. Much younger. I suppose you would say he was wet behind the ears. He overheard the old gunfighter and wanted to show him how fast he could draw. I thought we might have a shoot out right there in the train car."

"What happened?" Lindy sounded far too eager in Matt's mind.

Gwen glanced around the table, her gaze stalling at Matt. "The old guy sat down, crossed his arms, and said that was his past. He only cared about the present and where he'd get a good cup of coffee." She laughed, a cheerful sound.

Lindy joined in. Her laughter higher pitched but full of amusement that went right to the depths of Matt's heart. It was good to hear that sound.

"That's funny," she said.

The others also chuckled then they concentrated on the food.

Andy looked up from his plate. "There any more bread? Oh, I see it." He pushed back and went to the cupboard to cut several thick slices, keeping two for himself and putting the rest on the serving plate.

Riley waited until his brother sat down again then spoke to Gwen. "Tell us about yourself."

"What do you want to know?" Gwen's grin widened as if she had information that would amuse them.

"Did Matt say you have no family back east?"

Matt had told them very little about the woman he hoped to marry. Mostly because he didn't care to hear an opinion from any of them. Also, because he didn't know much.

"My parents died six years ago leaving me and my brother. I kept house for him until recently when he married." She glanced down at her plate, the only sign that her brother's marriage had cost her the only home she'd known since she was orphaned. "I needed to move on and the West beckoned. When Mrs. Ingram and Mrs. Strong set us together as being a compatible match for what we both wanted I knew this was the place for me. So far, they seem to be right."

Her answer silenced his brothers. Momentarily.

Luke cleared his throat before he spoke. "If you change your mind about him, I'll give you a home. You might like my house better'n his."

Gwen chuckled. "I think we'll do just fine together." She turned her steady gaze to Matt. "I believe my parents would approve of you."

Matt wasn't one to gloat. He left that up to his twin, but he felt a sudden urge to expand his chest and give a triumphant look.

"My mama and papa died when their wagon ran down a steep hill and crashed." Stunned silence followed Lindy's frank description of the accident. Who had even told her the details of her parents' deaths?

Lindy continued, unaware of how her statement had surprised them all. "They flew out like birds. Now they've flown right up to heaven. That's what Mrs. Ingram told me."

Gwen glanced around the table. Maybe she expected someone to respond to Lindy's words but Matt, for one, didn't know what to say. He knew his brothers and Wally were equally at a loss.

Gwen turned back to Lindy. "I understand heaven is a beautiful place."

Lindy bounced around in her chair to address Gwen. "Do they have birds there?"

Gwen wrapped her arm across Lindy's shoulders and ducked her forehead to Lindy's. "I don't know exactly what heaven is like, but I know God will provide everything we need to be perfectly happy."

Lindy nodded. "That's what Mrs. Ingram said."

Silence, as stiff and hollow as a reed, followed her words.

Wally was the first to recover and he pushed back. "I made peach cobbler for dessert. Don't expect anyone wants some."

"I do," Lindy yelled.

A short time later, the meal ended, and Gwen insisted on helping with the dishes. Lindy ran outside to play before anyone could suggest she should grab a towel and dry. Not that they expected her to work. She was, after all, only four. Though, in Matt's opinion, it was never too young to learn a little responsibility.

As soon as the kitchen was clean, Matt rose. "We'll be heading home."

Riley tipped back his chair. "Wait a minute. Haven't you forgotten something?"

Matt looked around. "I don't think so." His brothers and Wally all gave him dark looks but he could think of no reason.

Riley lowered his chair to all fours. "You didn't get married."

"I explained my decision."

"You won't be sleeping at your house." Why was Riley suddenly all big brother and bossy?

"Says who?" He bristled at being ordered around in that fashion.

"You didn't marry her." Riley spoke slowly as if dealing with a child.

Matt rubbed the back of his neck which had developed a painful knot. "As I recall, you told me I was acting prematurely to rush into a marriage."

"Yeah, I did but you ignored my advice."

"Riley, I took it. I decided to give us both"—he tipped his head to indicate he included Gwen—"opportunity to assess our decision."

Riley's hands bunched into fists. "Seems to me you left it a little too late."

Luke stood before Matt, his arms crossed, a scowl darkening his face. "Matt, have a thought for the girl's reputation."

Andy let out a long, impatient sigh.

Great. Now Matt was about to hear from his baby brother.

"Why didn't you leave her in town while you do this assessing and deciding?"

"I don't have time to run to town and visit her. Besides, how would that help with Lindy?" Each word burned his tongue. Mrs. Ingram had warned him against bringing Gwen to the ranch, but he hadn't expected opposition from his own family. In fact, he'd counted on them to support his decision. They were all honorable men. Gwen was safe with them. But they made it clear that wasn't enough.

The delay was only to see if she could handle Lindy before they made such an important decision. He had no need of or desire for a wife. Working during daylight hours left him only evenings to spend with Gwen, sharing Lindy's care, and assessing her abilities. Seems that wasn't going to happen if he cared about her reputation.

Now, what was he going to do?

4

Gwen kept her peace though she was prepared to suggest they return to Crow Crossing and get married thus solving this quandary. On the other hand, she was pleased to think there was concern for her reputation. Here she was on a ranch some distance from town and, as Mrs. Ingram had pointed out, surrounded by men. Lindy would hardly be considered as any sort of chaperone. Surely, Matt would see that marriage was the best solution.

Matt raked his fingers through his hair. "How are we supposed to learn about each other if she's over there and I'm here? That isn't going to work."

Wally shuffled over from where he'd been wiping the table. "Take the girl home. Lindy can stay there so she and Miss Gwen can get to know each other. You help her put Lindy to bed. Stay a while and talk. Then git yerself over here for the night." He flicked the wet rag at them. "How hard is that?"

"Guess that's all right," Riley allowed, crossing his arms and looking for all the world like a stubborn parent ready to separate the two of them.

Luke leaned toward Gwen, a wide grin claiming his lips. "You come running if you need someone to straighten him out. I'm an old hand at dealing with him."

Matt grabbed Gwen's elbow. "Let's get out of here before my brothers come up with any more hare-brained ideas."

Gwen trotted at his side out the door and down the path, laughing so hard, she had to stop partway to their house. She gasped for breath and wiped the tears from her eyes.

Matt studied her with narrowed eyes. "I'm not sure what's so funny."

Unable to speak, she shook her head. Her gaze jolted to his and her laughter choked off at the look in his eyes. She wasn't sure how to describe it. Perhaps surprise at her unexpected mirth or maybe a touch of approval as if he liked seeing and hearing her laugh. Whatever it was, she felt it clear to the bottom of her heart where it settled with a welcome warmth. As if she'd enjoyed a sweet cup of tea after a long, cold outing.

She blinked and slid her gaze away. She'd never been given to such fanciful thoughts and put it down to the strangeness of the situation.

"Ain't you home yet?" Wally's call from behind them broke the spell and they both hurried down the path until they reached the house.

"Where's Lindy?" she asked.

"I was wondering the same thing." He cupped his hands to his mouth and shouted her name.

They waited as Gwen eyed the nearby bushes, the trees, and Shannon Valley. She'd glimpsed the barn and some animals as they drove up to the house. How was she to keep a child safe amidst all these possible dangers? *Calm down. Lindy has lived here all her life and is no doubt well aware of what was appropriate. She'd likely find city life held much more risk.*

"Lindy!" Matt bellowed again.

The little girl came running, her arms flapping like featherless wings.

She skidded to a halt in front of them and balanced on her toes. "My name is Yellow Bird." Her voice was squawky as she pretended to be a bird.

Amusement, intermingled with a fondness for the child, swelled inside Gwen's chest. Lindy had an irrepressible spirit that she admired.

"Time to come in." Matt opened the door and stepped aside.

Lindy rocked back and forth on her toes, her fingers in her armpits as she continued to flap. "Yellow Bird not like going in house. Yellow Bird scared."

Gwen beckoned with her finger. "Come on, Yellow Bird. There's a nice warm nest here for you."

Matt rolled his eyes and leaned against the door frame. Gwen could tell he didn't have a lot of patience with the child's delay. But Gwen understood Lindy was expressing her fears at the change before her, and she spoke to Matt. "I think Yellow Bird would like some bedtime stories."

Lindy wagged her head up and down. "Yellow Bird like to read new story book."

"By all means." Gwen swooped her hand in a large welcome and Lindy darted in. "Yellow Bird will have to wear a nightgown to hear the story."

Lindy hesitated. Then dropped her arms as if she'd tired of the bird persona and marched into her room. The sound of drawers opening and closing informed Gwen and Matt that she was preparing for bed.

Gwen would have liked to help her but wasn't sure if the child was ready for that so waited in the living room.

Lindy returned wearing a nightdress that twisted about her body. Her hair flew out in every direction. Gwen ached to brush the mop of hair and braid it, to smooth the nightie and hug the little girl. Lindy pressed the new book to her chest and looked uncertainly from one adult to the other.

"Would you like me to read it?" Gwen asked. "Or would you prefer Uncle Matt?"

Lindy's gaze went from one to the other. Gwen felt

her longing and uncertainty so keenly it stung her eyes. "Or we could all sit on the settee with you in the middle."

Lindy nodded and climbed into place. Gwen sat on one side of her and Matt on the other. The adults looked at each other. His message was clear, and she hoped hers was too. Lindy must be allowed to choose how and when she would accept the new situation.

Lindy moved the book to Matt's leg. "You read it."

Matt opened the pages and began to read *Polly and the North Star*. He gave Gwen a look so ripe with what-kind-of-story-is-this that she sucked in her lips to keep from laughing. Gwen had thought the story was good and the pictures wonderful.

He shook his head and turned back to the book. He read:

Polly liked the sky, especially at night. Her papa said the stars might be angels watching over us.

Polly wished she could meet one of those angels. Maybe they would teach her to fly, and she could become a star, but Papa said angels didn't do that.

Matt's deep voice and the soft cadence of his words soothed Gwen. She prayed it would do the same for Lindy.

"You can only get your wings and learn to fly when you get to heaven. But it's nice to think how many angels there are. God sends them to help us."

Polly knew Papa had more to say and listened carefully.

"Sometimes they go ahead of us to guard our path.

57

Sometimes they talk to God about what we need. Sometimes they even visit us without us knowing it which is why we should be kind to strangers. They also sing around the throne of God. What a wonderful song that must be."

Polly climbed to her papa's knees. "How do you know about angels?"

Papa said, "Because God tells us about them in the Bible."

"I wish I had my own angel."

Papa took her out in the yard and pointed to the sky. "See that bright star? It's the North Star. It's like your own angel. You can look up anytime in the night and it's always there."

Polly looked at the star for a long time. "It's so far away. And I can't see it in the daytime."

Papa picked her up in his strong arms. "Maybe God uses it to remind us that He is always with us even when we can't see Him. He never changes. His heart is always shining with love for us."

And the Lord, He it is that doth go before thee; He will be with thee, He will not fail thee, neither forsake thee: fear not, neither be dismayed. Deuteronomy 31:8

Matt finished with Lindy leaning over his legs looking at the pictures of a star-filled sky. His dour expression gave the impression he wasn't impressed with the story but couldn't deny it held Lindy's attention.

Lindy put the book on Gwen's leg. "Now you read it."

"My pleasure." She read the words slowly, letting Lindy dwell on the pictures, and prayed the child would be comforted by the thought of stars and angels and God's unfailing love.

MATT LISTENED to Gwen read the story. He could almost imagine her voice coming from the sky, one of the angels speaking softly and calmly, filling the room with a sense of peace and comfort. Maybe the book wasn't as inappropriate as he first thought it to be. He knew Gwen to be a believer. It had been one of the first questions he'd asked. Mrs. Ingram had assured him that her friend back in Illinois vouched for Gwen's Christian faithfulness. Nevertheless, he'd had qualms about the theology expressed, but on the last page, he'd seen the list of scriptures supporting the story.

Lindy was fascinated with the book. The pictures of star-filled skies were beautiful. One reminded him of a famous painting he'd once seen on display. Only a copy, mind you. There were illustrations of angels… guarding children on a bridge, an angel in the sky. There was something familiar about that one.

As Gwen read the story, he suddenly remembered where he'd seen the picture before. It was one of the illustrations in his mother's Bible. Well, this whole business must be all right if one image had been there.

He smiled at his faulty reasoning. And yet it changed his mind about the story.

Lindy turned her face up and studied Gwen.

"I like this book. Thank you."

Gwen cupped her hand around Lindy's head. "I'm glad and you're welcome."

Lindy turned back to the page open on Gwen's knee and touched the picture.

Matt was about to ask the child what she was thinking when she closed the book.

"It's time for you to go to bed," Gwen said. "Can I tuck you in?"

Matt held his breath. He should have warned Gwen that Lindy had refused to let him—indeed, any of them—accompany her to bed since her parents' deaths.

"Sure." Lindy got to her feet and waited for Gwen to accompany her.

Matt stared after them a moment. "Can I come?"

Lindy shook her head. "Just Auntie Gwen."

He sat back, trying not to take her refusal personally. From the bedroom came the murmur of their voices. A few minutes later, Gwen returned to the living room and sat on a wooden chair across from him.

"She's already asleep."

"She hasn't slept well since...well, since the accident. She often wanders around in the night."

Gwen's gaze went to the bedroom. "Poor child."

"She hasn't let anyone help her into bed either." Matt didn't know if he was surprised by Lindy's choice or maybe a little put out that she would allow a stranger to tuck her in but not her Uncle Matt whom she'd known all her life.

"I'm glad she let me." Gwen's gaze circled the room. "Do you have any objection to me decorating the house as I wish?"

"None at all." But he wasn't ready to change the subject so completely. "Where did you find that book you gave her?"

"At a bookstore back in Kellom. Do you disapprove?"

He shook his head. He hadn't meant for uncertainty to creep into his voice. "I wasn't sure what to think at first. But that one picture where the angel is reaching out to touch a sick man...well, I recognize it from my mother's Bible."

Gwen smiled. "That's nice."

He nodded. What had become of his mother's Bible? It must be in the big house somewhere.

"Tell me about your mother. All you said was she died nine years ago. You'd have been sixteen at the time. Am I right?"

The illustration and Gwen's words triggered a flood of memories. "She was a patient woman. Pa could sometimes be careless about things. I remember one time...." He stopped. He hadn't thought of that particular incident in years and wasn't sure now was an appropriate time to mention it.

"I'd like to hear." Gwen's voice was gentle, inviting.

It was a memory he'd never told anyone, but in the interest of getting to know each other better, he should tell her. Besides, it threatened to explode from his thoughts. "I haven't remembered this in years but one day I saw my ma crying because Pa tracked mud all over her clean floors. She didn't know I saw her. She hurried to her room. I watched through the crack in the door. She fell to her knees and cried softly. Then she murmured some words."

He remembered them as clearly as the day he'd heard them. "'Lord, I know he doesn't mean to overlook the things I do. But sometimes I get tired of not being noticed. I grow weary of my work being of no importance to him. Truth is, I'm tired.'" He swallowed audibly, the memory carrying more power than he expected.

He forced himself to continue, grateful he was able to keep his voice strong. "She pulled her Bible close and ran her finger along the page. After a bit, she said, 'Yes, Lord. Not my will but thine.' I hurried away lest she discovers me spying on her." How could he have forgotten the impact of observing her?

He continued. "I learned a worthy lesson. Don't overlook the good things people do. I was naturally neat and organized but after that, I went out of my way to be so, and I often commented on things Ma had done. I said I appreciated the bread she'd baked. I thanked her for fixing our clothes for Sunday. I noticed and said so when she cleaned the porch of winter muck." He'd promised himself not to overlook what others did for him. He'd forgotten that over the years. He could change that right now. "Thank you for bringing that book for Lindy and reading it to her. Thank you for coming out and taking a chance on the unknown."

Her eyes widened then crinkled at the corners. Her pleasure spread across her face like the dawn of a new day. She chuckled. "You're welcome. And I thank you for offering me a home and a child to take care of." Her smile flattened and her eyes darkened. He felt the intensity of her study clear to the pit of his stomach.

Then she drew in a long breath and shifted her attention past him. "I truly like what I've seen of your ranch. I'm already fond of Lindy." Her gaze returned to him. "But I'm not sure what to expect in the coming days."

She was asking for a schedule. He certainly approved of that. "Lindy's an early riser and likes to be outside most of the day."

"What about meals?"

He blinked. "I assumed you would cook."

She chuckled. "I assure you I make excellent meals. But is Wally going to expect us?"

He didn't know her well enough to be certain, but it sounded like she wouldn't like that. "Tonight, he only took on the chore because of the circumstances. Normally, the three of us would eat here."

"Good. We need to function as a family. What time do you want breakfast?"

"Umm." His throat tightened at the thought. He wanted a mother for Lindy and taking a wife had seemed the best solution. A marriage in name only. To guarantee permanency. He wanted nothing to do with anything more. Corine's death had shattered his heart. Losing his parents and then Roscoe and Merry guaranteed it would never mend. But sitting at the table, watching Gwen—and Lindy, of course—offered something that beckoned him and, at the same time, rattled the walls around his heart. It suggested something he'd once enjoyed.

He dismissed the foolish thoughts, said good night, and returned to the main house. Luke and Riley had gone to their homes, Wally to his cabin, and Andy to the room he'd had since the house was built. Matt went to the room he'd once shared with Luke, grateful not to be questioned or teased.

He tried to recall what Gwen had said to his offer of marriage in name only. Having her letters with him, he pulled them from the valise and read them again by the light of the lamp. She'd agreed to his offer. Said she wanted a home and being married assured her that it'd be permanent. But she hadn't been the one to say it would be in name only. That was him. All him. He put the letters away. A marriage of convenience still seemed best. They could share a home, take care of Lindy and keep their feelings out of the business. Seemed the surest way to make sure no one got hurt.

He realized nothing more had been said about a routine or schedule. He would remedy the matter at breakfast.

How was Gwen managing Lindy? Would she waken if the child took to wandering in the night? He'd warned her but had he been clear enough? He would not forgive himself, nor overlook Gwen's failings if Lindy wandered out into the dark.

See, this was the rationale behind his decision to delay the wedding for a month. He had to make sure this was the right thing to do. For Lindy's sake.

And Gwen's, of course. After all, she was a city girl who might find ranch life did not suit her. Far better to learn that before they made a commitment.

He, Matthew Shannon, only wanted someone to care for his house and the child. Someone he could live with in peace. He did not need or want anything more. Certainly not love. Experience had taught him it left him vulnerable. And powerless.

He did not care to repeat that feeling.

5

$\mathcal{G}$ wen lay awake a long time, the silence intense. An occasional intruding, unfamiliar sound was like a trumpet blare. Someone or something coughed, and she jerked upright. Then came a moo. A cow, she assured herself. Just a cow. She hadn't expected to be sleeping alone—apart from a young child—in a strange house. Would any of the men hear her if she called for help?

She smiled into the darkness. It was hard to believe that Luke and Matt were twins. They didn't look alike nor act alike. Luke seemed to be a tease while Matt was...

She cupped her hands beneath her head. How would she describe him to someone? Like Maurice. She'd write her brother in the morning and let him know she'd arrived safely. Perhaps she wouldn't tell him yet that they weren't married. Maurice would be shocked to know her living situation. But as she'd said to him when she announced she was heading west, they had to move on, each in their own direction and this was the route she had chosen.

He'd wanted her to explain why she would go so far away and to strangers. All she could say was it seemed best to make a clean break. How could she tell him that she didn't want to watch Patricia take over the house that had been Gwen's for six years? How could she explain how devastated she was by losing her home without hurting him? And she didn't wish to do that. A new start in a new locale, with the promise of forever, seemed best.

She was determined she would still get the marriage she'd been offered.

A sound jerked her from her reminiscing. She strained toward it and decided it was the wind through the trees causing a sigh and murmur. She focused on the task ahead. A month? She would prove to be such a good mother and homemaker that Matt wouldn't be able to think of life without her.

Her first impressions of Matt were that he was a man who liked routine and order. Perhaps more than she cared about, but she could accommodate him. She could organize the pantry like he wanted. She could keep a schedule if he so desired. But shouldn't she put Lindy's needs ahead of his wants? She had so many plans for the child. How she would play with her, read to her, and enjoy her company. Surely Matt wouldn't object to that.

She liked the child. Sweet. Innocent. Gwen smiled thinking of how Lindy pretended she was flying. The book Gwen had chosen had been well received. *Lord, help me find ways to help her and befriend her. This has to be very strange for her. Comfort her.*

THE NEXT MORNING Gwen wakened early to the sound of birds singing outside her window. She hurriedly dressed and went to the kitchen. There was no lack of supplies for making meals.

Lindy raced into the room and dropped to the nearest chair. "What's for breakfast? I'm hungry."

Gwen laughed. "Good morning to you too. How did you sleep?"

"Good. Uncle Matt likes pancakes and eggs. So do I."

"Then we shall have that. How would you like to help?"

Lindy's eyes lit. "Can I? Uncle Wally won't let me. He says I make a mess. But Mama always let me."

"Maybe Uncle Wally is so efficient he doesn't need assistance, but I sure do. Why don't you find me a bowl for the batter?"

Lindy was off her chair and rooting through the cupboards before Gwen finished.

"I might have seen bowls in the pantry." Gwen followed Lindy to the shelves.

Lindy chose a suitable dish and held it toward Gwen, but Gwen waved it away. "Put it on the table." A worktable stood beneath a long narrow window. "Now measure out the flour."

Lindy dipped a cup into the flour and dumped the contents into the bowl. A bit fell to the floor and Lindy stopped, looking to Gwen for her reaction.

"It's just flour. We can sweep it up when we're done."

Lindy ducked her head but not before Gwen saw the surprised and pleased smile on her face. She guided the little girl in measuring more flour and helped her add the baking powder. Her hand over Lindy's, they beat eggs and added them along with milk. It was nice to have a good supply of both. The batter ready, they moved to the stove where Gwen put a griddle to heat. Under her careful assistance, she allowed Lindy to turn the first batch of pancakes then suggested the child set the table while Gwen broke eggs into a frying pan.

Lindy put out plates. The cutlery was haphazard, but she'd done it by herself and returned to the chair by the stove. "Can I cook some more pancakes?"

"Surely."

The child chattered as she worked. "Papa said Mama made the best pancakes in the whole world. Do you think Uncle Matt will say that about mine?

Didcha know Uncle Luke uses syrup and jam both even though Uncle Wally says it's a waste? Uncle Wally pretends he's annoyed but I don't think he is. Do you?"

"Probably not." Gwen chuckled at Lindy's chatter.

The door opened and Matt stepped into the room. He studied them, his eyebrows twitching. Gwen lifted the child down and handed her a plate of pancakes.

"Look what I made for you, Uncle Matt." Lindy carefully placed the plate on the table.

Gwen took over carrying the rest of the food. She filled two cups with coffee. There was milk for Lindy. Gwen sat beside Lindy with Matt across the corner. His troubled eyes rested on her for several seconds before he cleared his throat.

"I'll ask the blessing." He bowed his head.

Gwen did so as well, slowly, and thoughtfully. She wasn't sure what she'd done to displease him and hoped he wouldn't tell her in front of Lindy. The words of his prayer didn't register with her. But at his *amen*, she sprang to action and held the platter of eggs toward him.

He took three and then helped himself to the pancakes Lindy offered. The child waited while he slathered on butter, poured on thick syrup, and cut a generous forkful. He chewed the portion and nodded. "These are good, Lindy."

She beamed. "As good as Mama's?"

"I'd say so."

Lindy sat back. "Mama was a good cook, wasn't she?"

Matt's look was warm as he answered her. "She was the best."

Gwen smiled as she turned her attention to the food. It was good to see the child happy.

A few minutes later, Matt took the last pancake and wiped his plate clean with it. "Is everyone done?" he asked.

Lindy nodded and he addressed her. "Then you can run out and play while I talk to Auntie Gwen."

Lindy was gone in a flash, her arms outspread like wings.

Something about Matt's tone warned her he had orders for her. She pulled her shoulders back and lifted her chin. Whatever he wanted, she would do her best to obey. She had to prove she could live up to his standards and would make a worthy wife...someone he couldn't manage without. No changing his mind when he discovered her failings. She grinned to herself. Not that she was going to admit to any.

Matt cleared his throat. "We didn't get around to talking about a routine."

Routine? That wasn't so bad. She nodded. "Tell me what you expect."

"First off. I don't think a four-year-old should be working at the stove."

Gwen barely managed to hold back a protest. She

breathed deeply. *Be calm. Be reasonable.* "Lindy told me her mama let her do so."

"Oh." Stunned silence that lasted a heartbeat. "If Merry thought it was all right…"

She waited for him to continue. But it seemed like he'd forgotten to tell her what he thought. "When do you expect meals to be served?"

"Breakfast is at seven. I like to eat after the chores are done. Dinner at twelve. We always stop whatever we're doing and come to the house to eat. It's something Ma and Pa always did. Merry always had the meal ready when we walked in. Supper…well, it depends on what we're doing. Normally, around six. But if we're going to be later, I'll let you know."

"That sounds fine."

"Merry always did laundry on Monday. She'd had the clotheslines full before breakfast."

"Heavens. Did she get up in the middle of the night?" Gwen hadn't meant to sound so surprised.

Matt's brows knotted. "She was very efficient. The woman never wasted a moment."

"Good to know." It was plain as the nose on his face that he expected the same from Gwen.

"She baked twice a week. We always had bread, cookies, and dessert. You can ask Wally for recipes if you need help."

It was a good thing Matt couldn't see how Gwen bristled. "I've taken care of my brother for six years. I think I can manage."

"Don't be too prideful to ask for help."

She breathed in until her lungs almost burst then spoke calmly. "Of course, I won't."

"As I already mentioned, I'd like to see Lindy having more order in her life."

Gwen was thoroughly confused. "I don't know what you mean. What sort of order should she have?"

His eyes narrowed. Perhaps her tone gave away more of her irritation than she meant to reveal. But she honestly didn't know what he expected, and she couldn't imagine regimenting the child like a little soldier.

She swallowed hard. Proving herself to be amiable and satisfactory might be more of a challenge than she anticipated.

 * * *

THERE WAS no need for Matt to rush out after breakfast as he'd done the chores already. That gave him time to set out his expectations regarding Lindy. He'd mulled around what he wanted. He'd produced what he thought were reasonable guidelines. "We were taught to do simple tasks at her age. I propose that she take the kitchen scraps to the chickens and get the eggs."

Gwen nodded.

Good. No disagreement so far. Nor should there be. Her job was to take care of Lindy. His was to be sure it was done right...the way Roscoe and Merry would want their daughter raised. "She's certainly old enough to help with dishes. Merry had her doing so. She could make her bed and keep her room tidy."

Gwen seemed interested in the plate before her. Was she anxious to get on with her work? He couldn't fault her in that. Not that he sought ways to do so.

She lifted her head. Her eyes were dark. "I'd like to take her for walks, but I need to know where she's allowed to go and what's safe for her. I'm a city girl so I'm not familiar with what's expected on a ranch. Now if we were in town, I would warn her about crossing the street and staying away from horses. I'd not let her wander around without supervision."

"How'd it be if I show you around? Shall I return in, say half an hour?" That would give her time to clean the kitchen and do the dishes.

Gwen pushed to her feet. "That would be good."

He grabbed his hat and headed down the path. Riley had informed him that they were going to ride out to check on the herd and their cowhands. Matt stepped into the main house.

Riley stood before him, his cowboy hat in his hands. "You ready to go?" Luke and Andy were at his back.

"I'm going to need a bit of time to show Gwen around, so she knows where it's safe for her and Lindy to go."

Luke whoofed with amusement. "Lindy knows. Let her do it."

Riley planted his hat on his head. "We need to be on our way."

Wally joined them, handing a sack to Andy. It was food for the day which wouldn't last until noon if Andy oversaw it.

Riley reached for the sack. "I'll take that."

Andy gave it up with a muttered protest.

Matt and Luke looked at each other and chuckled. Sometimes it was nice to have a twin who understood what he was thinking without him saying it.

Matt returned his attention to Riley. "It won't take long."

Riley sighed heavily. "I suppose we can wait a few minutes. Luke can saddle your horse to save time."

Luke groaned. "Why do I always get stuck with his work?"

"Because you're my twin." Matt stepped from the house. "Where's Lindy? I want her to come too so there's no misunderstanding."

Riley looked at the other two and they all laughed.

"You're going to try and clip the wings on that little girl? I can't wait to see how that goes," Luke said.

Matt ignored them as he headed for the barn. Their dog, Scamp, stayed there when he wasn't working, and Lindy often spent time with him. There was a mother cat and three kittens in the loft. Another of her favorite places. She had more places she sought out, but he wasn't even sure where they were as she would appear out of nowhere when he called.

"Lindy." He raised his voice. She'd hear if she were nearby.

She darted from the barn. "Yes?"

"We're going to show Auntie Gwen around." He held out his hand, but she skipped ahead, her arms wide. Did the child never grow tired of holding her arms aloft?

They reached his house. Before he could open the door, Gwen stepped out, her face alight with excitement. "I can't wait to see everything."

Lindy took Gwen's hand as they walked beside Matt. His intention was to return to the barn and corrals, but he realized there were other things he needed to point out.

"Shannon Valley has steep banks. There is a trail down to the bottom. I'll show it to you someday."

"I'm not 'posed to go there," Lindy announced airily.

"That's right." He turned his attention back to Gwen. "She can't go into Riley or Luke's houses without permission from them. She knows that, don't you, Lindy?"

"Nothing there anyway." She spoke with such disgust that he knew she'd inspected each thoroughly. With permission, of course. At least he hoped so.

"What about the big house?" Gwen paused. The place in question was dead ahead.

"She's had the run of the place." But things had changed. "However, Lindy, I don't want you going in unless Uncle Wally or Uncle Andy is there."

She ground to a halt, jammed her little fists to her nonexistent hips, and glowered at him. "That's my house, you know. I live there."

"Not any—"

Gwen's hand pressing to his arm cut his words off. She shook her head just enough for him to understand she didn't think he should continue. He clamped his lips together. He didn't expect her to argue with everything he said. Though to be accurate, she hadn't said a word. Nor did she need to.

Lindy raced away, flying into the house.

Matt took a step after her.

Her hand still on his arm, Gwen stopped him again. "She needs time to adjust to this change."

He shook her hand off and hurried after the child with Gwen on his heels. He'd known Lindy since she was born. Her parents had been his best friends. How could Gwen think she knew more about what Lindy needed than he did?

The sound of doors banging led him to the little bedroom that had been Lindy's since her birth. It was a nursery off her parents' bedroom. He paused at the doorway and stared at the bed where Roscoe and Merry had slept together as husband and wife. And now they were gone. He ground his teeth and crossed to where Lindy opened and closed dresser drawers with a shuddering slam.

"See. My things are here." Her jaw trembled along with her shoulders.

He should have thought to take everything over before now. "We need to take them to your new room."

She slammed the drawer so hard it bounced open again. She slammed it again and again.

Gwen sat on the little cot. "Lindy, you don't need to move your things unless you want to."

Lindy sank to the floor and pulled her knees to her chest.

Matt strode from the house. How dare Gwen defy him before the child?

The others sat in their saddles watching him. Scamp bounced eagerly at the heels of the horses. The dog did like to work. Matt's own mount was ready to ride. He jumped to the saddle and reined about. "What's taking you fellas so long?" He galloped from the yard.

Luke was the only one who kept up with him. The other two sauntered along at a leisurely pace. Huh. *So much for we gotta get the work done.*

Luke hollered at him. "See you didn't make it to the barn. You sure she'll be safe? Maybe she'll take in her mind to ride a bull. Or jump from the loft. Or—"

"She's not an idiot," Matt yelled.

"Seems you should be telling yourself that." Luke fell back and left Matt to gallop ahead on his own.

Was his twin suggesting he treated Gwen like she was an idiot?

What did Luke know? What did Gwen know? Matt wasn't even sure what he wanted any longer. Except a woman to take care of Lindy. He just hadn't imagined the woman might have ideas opposing his.

He slowed his horse and waited for the others to catch up. No way was he going to say anything about what had happened. The last thing he wanted was all their rag tail suggestions about what he should do.

He knew without their input. But was he going to do it?

Good thing he would be gone most of the day. It'd give him time to think. And give Gwen far too much time to explore on her own. Who knew what kind of trouble she'd get herself into? He should have taken the time to ask Wally to keep an eye on her.

His own words echoed in his head. She wasn't an idiot. But his insides did not relax, and they wouldn't until he returned home and saw for himself that she and Lindy were both safe and sound.

What had he gotten himself into?

Gwen looked at the empty doorway Matt had strode from. She'd displeased him. She shouldn't have interfered with his decision to move Lindy's clothing and belongings to his house. At the least, she should have asked him before she spoke to the child. Sensing Lindy's distress, she'd acted from her heart, wanting to assure Lindy it wasn't their intent to take her from what was familiar. Moving to Matt's house must feel like she was being ripped from the only home she'd ever known. There was no reason they couldn't wait for her to feel comfortable with the changes that had been thrust into her life.

On one hand, she regretted her action. She'd never convince Matt she was what he wanted for a wife, or more correctly, a mother for Lindy, if she kept opposing him. But she'd done the right thing for the child. She'd explain it to Matt if he'd give her a chance. But she'd watched him ride away with the others and knew he'd be gone all day.

Outdoors, she almost spread her arms out like Lindy did and twirl around. To not be on display…on trial, was freeing. But she wasn't a child, and she lowered her arms and settled for a quiet laugh. Then she slowly turned full circle. She was alone apart from Wally whom she'd seen disappear into the little cabin. And Lindy.

And the unknown.

She hadn't been to the barn. Hadn't been told where it was safe to go except not to Shannon Valley. At least he'd said he would take her down the trail at a later date.

Lindy came from the house, running and flapping

her arms. It appeared she'd forgotten her upset.

"Come on." Lindy reached for her hand. "I'll show you my cat. She has three kittens. Their eyes are just opening. They are sooooo cute."

Cute? It was a word Gwen seldom heard. Where had Lindy learned it? Her parents perhaps. She let Lindy lead her into the barn. As she stepped through the door, she inhaled deeply. The aroma was sharp and at the same time, calming. She nudged a pile of hay and a sweet, almost spicy smell hit her. She stood in a wide alleyway. On either side were wooden gates and dividers. The tops of each sturdy wooden bar were worn down by something.

"Lindy, why are the boards so uneven looking?"

"Oh that. The horses chew on them when they're bored. Come on. Let's go see Cat."

Gwen let Lindy drag her onward to a side alley where she came face to face with a ladder attached to the wall, leading to the floor overhead. She sucked in the musty air of the barn and held it in her lungs as Lindy scampered up the rungs. At the top, Lindy peered over the edge.

"You coming?" she called.

To see the child peering down, Gwen's heart jolted to her throat and hung there. It didn't seem safe. "Are you allowed to be up there?"

"Sure. It's where the cats are. How else would I see them? Come on."

A four-year-old had no trouble ascending. Joining

her shouldn't be a big challenge to an adult. But Gwen couldn't force her limbs to move. She must not let Lindy know how much she did not want to do this. She grabbed a wooden rung and shook it. The wood didn't budge, offering reassurance that the rung would hold her weight. She'd sooner it had provided her an excuse to refuse to go any further.

She lifted a foot to the first bit of wood. Her shoe caught in the hem of her skirt. She forced herself to release one hand and pull the fabric free. But that left her having to do the same for the next step. And there was no way she would let go of her handhold once she got several feet from the ground. She grabbed her skirt and palmed it and lifted her foot to the next rung.

Now off the solid floor of the barn, she stared at the stained wood before her, sucked in feeble courage, and lifted a foot to the next rung. And then the next. She was at eye level with the surface of the loft. "Where are the cats?" She could see them fine right here without letting go of the solid rungs.

"They's over there. You gotta come and see them." Lindy stood back, expectant, and impatient.

I can do this. I must do this. Gwen looked around for something to cling to. There was a wooden crossbar above her. If she stretched…. She eased up one more step, grabbed for the stud, and clung to it as she found footing.

"Come on." Lindy took her hand and half dragged her forward. In the corner, on an old rug amidst a mound of hay lay a cat with three kittens. The mama cat meowed a welcome to Lindy who fell to her knees and rubbed mama cat's chin. She lifted one of the kittens. "You can hold this one if you want."

Gwen accepted the tiny creature. The solid gray kitten meowed weakly. She pressed her cheek to the silky fur.

Loneliness ached through her at the memories flooding her heart. Her cat—Silky—was gone by now. She knew Patricia had made Maurice promise to destroy Gwen's pet as soon as she left. The only thing about that decree that surprised her was that Patricia didn't insist on it while Gwen was still there.

Silky had been bigger than this kitten when Mama and Gwen brought her home. Mama loved cats too. Gwen closed her eyes and drew in slow deep breaths to hold her sorrow at bay.

There was no point in dwelling on the past. She was beginning a new life.

"That one is named Stormy." Lindy lifted the second kitten. It was gray with white and orange areas. "This one is Patches." She put the kitten in her lap and picked up the third one which was black with a white nose and white paws. "This one is Mittens."

"Perfect names. What's mama cat's name?"

"She's Cat."

"Cat?"

"That's what Papa always called her. 'Where's Cat? Here, take some milk to Cat. Cat caught a mouse for you.'" She giggled at that and then concentrated on the kittens in her lap. "Papa will never see them get big, will he?"

Gwen sat beside Lindy on the dusty floor. "Your papa liked cats, didn't he?"

Lindy nodded. Gwen tried to think how best to reassure the child. She'd suffered a horrible loss. One that a four-year-old couldn't begin to understand. Death was so final. Even knowing one's parents were in a better place did not ease the pain. She remembered her own struggles and spoke from the heart.

"Lindy, honey, I think I'm right in saying your papa would want you to enjoy the kittens as much as he would have. I believe he is sorry he didn't get a chance to tell you goodbye before he left. But God surrounded you with people who love you and will take care of you."

Lindy silently stroked the kittens. After a moment, she turned her face toward Gwen. "Did God send you to take care of me?"

Gwen hugged the child, her heart bursting with love. "I believe so and I'm so very happy He did."

Lindy pursed her lips, her expression sober. "I am too."

Tears stung Gwen's eyes at those words. Whatever it took to earn Matt's approval she would do. And not just to secure a home for herself, but more importantly, to provide Lindy with the love she needed.

One by one, Lindy put the kittens back with Cat

and got to her feet. Gwen stood at her side, waiting to see what she wanted to do next. With a whoop of joy, the child ran a few steps and then slid the rest of the way across the floor. "Come on, Auntie Gwen, it's fun."

"Only if you're little." She moved toward the gaping hole in the floor, prepared to catch Lindy if she slid too close. She wanted to tell her to stop but she couldn't let her own fears dictate what the child did.

Lindy skidded to a halt in front of Gwen. "You wanna see more?"

Gwen put her hand on Lindy's shoulder to hold her back from the opening. Shaking away her fears, she reveled in the pleasure of Lindy's offer.

"I'd love to."

Lindy shifted past Gwen and before Gwen could protest, scampered down the ladder. "Come on, Auntie Gwen."

Gwen gritted her teeth and edged toward the hole. It was a long way down, but she didn't intend to do it in one step. She grabbed the brace she'd used previously and with every nerve in her body screaming a protest, she lowered one foot and then the other to the first rung. Realizing she needed to move down even more so she could cling to one of the narrow cross pieces of wood, she sucked her lips in, closed her eyes, and moved her foot. It hit air. Her heart froze within her. *Pull it closer to the wall. You can do this.*

It took more courage than she knew she had to release her handhold and grasp the lower bar. But she did and slowly made her way to the barn floor where she sucked in musty yet refreshing air.

Lindy grabbed her hand and together they ran from the barn, their footsteps thudding. They reached the bright sunlight. Gwen blinked and laughed at the sheer relief at having her feet on solid ground.

"Where are we going?" she asked the child who continued to tug at her arm.

"You wanna see the garden?"

"Yes, please." She'd seen the houses and the insides of two, but she'd like to see what else constituted the ranch buildings and yard.

Lindy tugged on her hand. They passed the corner of the barn where a horse nickered a greeting. A cow lifted her head and regarded them a second then resumed grazing. A long, narrow building stood past the corrals.

Gwen slowed her steps. "What's that?"

"Where the cowboys live when they're here. Right now, they're with the cows. That's where Uncle Matt and Uncle Luke, Uncle Riley and Uncle Andy went today."

"And the building beside it?"

"Where they eat."

Eat? That meant cooking. "Who cooks the meals?"

Lindy stopped to stare at the structure. "Boots. But I have to call him Mr. Boots. He lives in the eating house and doesn't like little girls bothering him."

"Then I'm guessing you aren't allowed to go to the

cookhouse." She knew that's what the place was called.

Lindy rocked back and forth and stared at the place. "You wanna see it?"

"Lindy, aren't you supposed to stay out of there?"

She continued to rock. "Mr. Boots isn't here."

Gwen would love to see inside and get a glimpse at how real cowboys lived. But she couldn't let Lindy be disobedient. She'd have to wait for someone else to show her. "That doesn't change the rules." She turned away from looking at temptation. "I thought you were going to take me to the garden."

Lindy let out a long-suffering sigh. "It's over there." She indicated a fence and trudged in that direction.

Gwen tried to keep back a laugh and then gave up.

Lindy turned to study her with a curious look on her face. "What's funny?"

"Us."

Lindy squinted, silently demanding an explanation.

Gwen took her hand and continued toward the garden. A perfect place to explain her thoughts. "Have you learned about the Garden of Eden?"

"Where Adam and Eve lived? Mama told me that story."

"Do you recall how they had a beautiful garden?"

Lindy poked her fingers through the squares of wire of the fence and plucked off a deep-pink flower. "Mama had a picture of it. Lots of flowers."

"It had lots of everything. Did your mama tell you about the tree they weren't supposed to eat from?"

Lindy buried her nose in the flower. "But they did. Right?"

"That's correct. All the trees and flowers you could imagine, but they had to go to the one they were told not to go to." She turned back to look at the forbidden buildings. "All this land, lots of places to explore. Right? But where do we want to go?"

Lindy grinned. "Where we aren't 'posed to."

Gwen pulled Lindy to her side. "Sometimes it's hard to obey but you do, don't you?"

Lindy pressed against Gwen's leg. "Mostly. You want this flower?" She held it up to Gwen.

"Thank you, sweet child."

"Welcome. There's nothing here. Just plants. Uncle Wally pulls the weeds. Sometimes Mama helped him."

"But the plants produce food that tastes good." She studied the growing vegetables. If the weather cooperated there would be plenty of harvest from the verdant rows. She hoped she'd get a share to can and preserve. Rhubarb thrived in one corner. A row of flowers grew near the fence. Only a few were in blossom but the bright yellow and pink added color.

"I like peas. But not beans." Lindy shook her head so hard her hair sprayed out.

It was only hair, Gwen reminded herself. But how she'd like to tidy it. Instead, she responded to Lindy's comment. "Do you eat them when they're served?" She wondered if the child was forced to eat everything on her plate.

"I just say no thank-you and pass the bowl on."

Gwen laughed at her matter-of-fact response.

They moved on down the trail, by smaller buildings. Lindy importantly opened the doors and explained what each was—a storeroom with shelves full of supplies, all neatly arranged. Harness room—saddle trees that were mostly empty. Empty hooks for the most part but some harnesses hung from the others. The third shed held tools—shovels, axes, picks, saws—a great array. Again, placed in perfect order. Gwen wondered if all the Shannon men were this tidy or if Matt kept the sheds as neat as he expected the pantry to be.

They moseyed along, Lindy keeping up a running commentary. This was the place where she'd fallen and scraped her knee. Papa had put ointment on it. That was where Mama picked yellow flowers. That was where Mama and Papa went for walks. "Sometimes they took me. Sometimes they waited 'til I was in bed. Papa said it was so he could kiss Mama." Lindy covered her mouth and giggled.

Gwen laughed too. She was so enjoying this delightful child. But the sun was heading toward its zenith.

"It's time for us to go to the house and have dinner."

"Wanna see a shortcut?"

Gwen followed Lindy down a narrow path through a thicket of trees and bushes. They entered a small clearing. Gwen knew from the way the grass was flattened that Lindy had been here before.

Lindy stopped. "We can pretend it's our secret house."

"That's a lovely idea. What do we need?"

"A table and chairs. Maybe a curtain."

"Where would we get them?"

Lindy beckoned with her finger. "I show you."

Gwen followed her to a woodshed where Lindy examined logs and picked out those that were what she determined to be right. Gwen helped her carry them back to the clearing. It took several trips, but they soon had five in a tight circle to form a table and four laying sideways as stools.

Gwen sat on one of the chairs watching as Lindy gathered objects. What was the child doing?

Lindy placed four green leaves on the table. "Our plates." She gathered withered rose hips and tore leaves into tiny pieces and put some of each on the plates. She looked around and then dashed away.

Gwen waited, wondering if Lindy was coming back or had she lost interest? Before she could think if she should continue to wait or go to the house, the child trotted back, carrying an empty tin can holding three white flowers. She put the arrangement in the center of the wooden table.

"Mama loved these," she announced solemnly then

sat across from Gwen and pretended to eat. "You like my cooking?"

Gwen pretended as well. "It's very good. Thank you." She nodded toward the two empty spots. "Are you expecting company?"

Lindy's hands grew still. She blinked. Then burst to her feet. "Yellow Bird likes to fly." Spreading her arms, she raced down the trail.

Gwen rose more slowly as she realized Lindy had set places for her mama and papa. Pain pierced her heart to know how much Lindy missed her parents.

Maybe she could help Lindy still have a good time.

She returned to the house and gathered up food for a picnic. Crackers, cheese, and a tin of Andy's cherished peaches. She plucked a checkered dishtowel from the drawer and chose two plates from the cupboards. For a moment, she hesitated, wondering if she should take four plates but decided it felt too much like intruding into Lindy's private world.

Back at the clearing she spread the cloth over the log table and set out the food. "Lindy," she called. She heard the child humming...a bird-like sound. "Lindy, I've made us a picnic."

Lindy flapped into sight. "Yellow Bird hungry." She skidded to a halt as she saw the table. Then she dropped her arms to her side and walked sedately to the log seat across from Gwen.

"Shall I say grace?" Gwen hoped her voice indicated she'd be willing to let Lindy do so.

Lindy bowed her head and clasped her hands together.

Tears stung Gwen's eyes and clogged her throat. What a precious child. She managed to choke out a prayer, hoping Lindy wouldn't notice the hoarseness of Gwen's voice.

The little girl talked between bites. She knew a lot about birds and what she didn't know she'd made up. It seemed there were crows at a certain tree who talked to her. Lindy repeated the pretend conversation.

"They have babies now. Mama crow told the babies they had to stay in the nest. She and papa crow fly away to get food then come back. The baby crows whisper to each other 'cause they don't know if mama and papa will come back or if they fly away forever." She waved her arm over her head. "They might fly away so high they never come back."

It seemed Lindy had chosen a story that mirrored her own.

"Uncle Matt told me baby birds will soon fly away. I told him I was going to learn to fly." Lindy flapped her arms.

They lingered over the picnic as Lindy entertained Gwen with her imaginative tales.

"Miss? Miss?"

The call jerked Gwen to her feet. Goodness, she'd spent a large portion of the day with Lindy. Not that she regretted it. Wasn't it the very reason she was here? To mother the child?

But also to take care of meals and the home. And she dared not fail in either department.

She rushed toward the house. Wally stood at the door.

"I brought meat for you." He lifted the pot he held.

"Thank you."

"If you start it roasting now it will be ready for supper."

"I'll do that." She took the pot.

"How's the little one doing?" He nodded toward Lindy who ran and flapped down the trail.

Gwen chuckled. "She's such a delight. Full of life and imagination." She blinked back tears.

Wally patted her arm. "Matt did right to bring you here."

"That's very kind of you. I'll do my best to…" She didn't know how to finish. Was Wally even aware of Matt's expectations from this delay?

"Don't you let Matt's ways get under your skin. He's learned to be cautious. And it's not a bad way even though some might find it trying at times. Now, is there anything you need?"

He'd learned to be cautious? Because of overhearing his mother crying and praying and his decision to not be like his pa? Though he'd not come right out and said that. Certainly, losing his friends would shock him and make him want to control what he could. She knew so little about him. Were there other reasons? A broken heart? Disappointment in love? People showing little or no concern for his feelings?

Or was she only remembering some of her own reasons for thinking a marriage of convenience was the safest thing?

She pulled her thoughts back to the present. "Matt said he likes dessert. I thought of making a pie or two." It was one way she could show her worth and perhaps make him feel like he was valued. "Do you mind if I help myself to some rhubarb?"

"You take all you want. The garden is as much yours as anyone's."

Gwen wasn't about to believe that but thanked the man. She browned the roast and stuck it in the oven then called Lindy and they returned to the garden. Lindy skipped down the path between two rows of peas, singing a tuneless song about crows.

Gwen pulled only enough rhubarb for pies, leaving many red stalks. She'd see about preserving the remainder if no one objected to her doing so.

Back at the house, she made pie crust as Lindy played outside, often out of sight but returning often enough that Gwen didn't worry about her. She concentrated on baking suspecting how well she managed was part of how she'd be judged. Not that she worried about that. She was a good cook and had lots of experience with meal preparation.

Wait until Matt tasted her pie. She had often

received compliments on her baking—cookies, cakes, and pies.

The pies were in the oven. She checked the roast and then prepared vegetables for the meal. She glanced at the clock. It was time to set the potatoes to cook if Matt was to return at six. The sound of horse hooves informed her he would soon be there.

She checked the pies. The first was done. She was about to pull it from the oven when a scream from outdoors shattered the peace. The pies forgotten, she dashed out the door. The sound came from toward the clearing where they'd had a picnic and she raced in that direction. Lindy stood in the middle of the path, yelling, and roughing her hair.

Gwen caught her hands. "Lindy, what's wrong?"

Lindy screamed, "Bee. Bee in my hair." Her shrieks continued as she jerked free and rubbed her head.

"Stop. Let me look." Gwen had to contend with Lindy's flailing hands as she examined the child's head. She found a bee trapped in the tangles and freed it. "It's gone." She lifted Lindy in her arms and held her tight. "It's gone," she repeated.

Lindy wrapped her arms and legs around Gwen and held on, sobbing loudly.

Gwen rubbed her back and made soothing sounds. Lindy slowly quieted and Gwen made her way back to the house, Lindy clinging to her. The moment she stepped inside, she knew her meal was in trouble.

She eased Lindy to a chair. "There you go." If she

had time, she would brush the child's hair but that would have to wait.

She pushed the potatoes to a cooler spot hoping she could salvage them and opened the oven and bit back a groan. The pie was blackened beyond use. She pulled it out and stared at it.

At that inopportune moment, Matt strode in.

So much for proving she could present a satisfactory meal. She turned to face him. His scowl drew his eyebrows together in a way that informed her that he was not pleased. Laughter bubbled up her throat at the situation and she extended the pie toward him. "May I present to you a burnt offering?" At the deepening scowl on his face, she knew she'd said the wrong thing. He didn't understand that she was only trying to see the humor in her failure. "Never mind." She put the pie on the counter. "Not everything is ruined." Thank goodness for the second pie.

MATT CHEWED BACK SCOLDING WORDS. He'd come home with the intention of apologizing for his behavior earlier in the day only to find his meal burning, and Lindy looking as neglected as a street urchin. The sight completely unraveled all his good intentions. He tried to recapture the peace he'd found out riding. The sunshine had been warm but not hot. The cows were scattered into three different valleys, but the cowboys were watching them. Boots had given them a list of food they needed. All in all, he'd enjoyed the day.

Until now.

He'd been clear as to what he wanted when he sent for Gwen: a mother for Lindy and someone to take care of the house. She said she'd tended her brother's home for years. Was adding a child to her responsibilities so…so…unmanageable?

Words of criticism burned on his tongue. But he remembered how Pa's careless remarks had hurt Ma and choked them back.

Luke had warned Matt to give Gwen time to adjust. "Don't forget she's a city girl. There will be a lot for her to get used to. And you can be such a grouch when things aren't exactly as you want them."

Matt had protested that he was never a grouch. He'd determined no one could accuse him of such. And now he had to live up to that decision. He pushed aside his initial reaction. "It's not the end of the world." Glancing around the kitchen, he noticed only a few pieces of wood were left in the wood box. "I'll fill that while you finish making supper."

"Thank you," she called after him as he left the house.

There. He'd just proved Luke wrong. He wasn't a grouch.

When he returned with an armload of wood, food was set on the table. He washed his hands and sat at the end. Lindy sat across the corner from him with Gwen at her side. Seems this was to be their places. For some reason, he didn't care for the arrangement. But he couldn't think of why he should object. Maybe Luke was right. Matt was getting irritable.

He said grace, filled his plate, and asked how they'd spent the day.

Lindy bounced forward. "We had a picnic. I showed her the baby kittens and we 'splored."

Alarm bells rang inside Matt's head. Exploring. Where? He soothed his fears. Gwen might be a city girl, but she wasn't stupid. Nevertheless, there were dangers with which she was likely unfamiliar with.

He grew aware that Lindy waited with an eager expression and Gwen smiled though the smile didn't reach her eyes. Was she sensing his reaction? "It sounds like you had a fun day." He lifted his gaze to Gwen. "I never did finish showing you around. I'd be happy to do that after supper if you like."

Her smile lightened her entire face. "I'd like it very much."

Lindy huffed. "I showed her everything."

Gwen's laughter rang out and Matt saw the humor in Lindy's protest and chuckled. He met Gwen's eyes and felt something at their shared amusement. Not that he had any idea what the warmth in his chest meant. Only that it felt good to push aside his critical thoughts and see the happier side of something.

Maybe Luke was right. He'd grown...well, he'd never admit to *grouchy*.

Gwen brought him a slice of pie. He tasted it and his eyes rounded. "I've never cared much for rhubarb pie, but this is delicious. Thank you." So what if the other pie was black?

They finished and he pushed from the table. "We'll help with dishes, won't we, Lindy?"

"Sure." The three of them took dishes to the basin where Gwen washed. Lindy and Matt dried. The kitchen cleaned, he looked at the burnt pie on the cupboard.

"I could take it to Scamp. He'd enjoy it."

Gwen looked startled then grinned. The grin grew to a low chuckle. "Poor Scamp must be very hungry to be willing to eat this."

"Considering he likes to eat offal and roll in it, this will be the best dessert he's ever had."

She chortled delightfully.

His own grin came from deep within at being able to amuse her. The pie in one hand, he escorted Gwen and Lindy out the door. He would have gone along the bank of Shannon Valley and pointed out various things, but he needed to deal with the burnt food first, so they turned the other direction. He held his breath as they passed the main house, hoping Lindy wouldn't insist she run inside, but she skipped ahead, flapping her arms and humming. At the barn, he called Scamp and set the pie on the ground. Like he'd expected, the dog dug in, his hindquarters wriggling as he ate.

"See. What did I say? He's so happy he's practically dancing."

A low laugh rumbled in her throat and, grinning at his success, Matt led her into the barn. "I know you were here with Lindy but let me explain things." He told her about dealing with horses. "We break our own."

She shuddered. "Break is such a harsh word."

"It's just a term. You might say we train them. From a young age, they are handled. We want them to trust us." He led her to the pasture behind the barn and pointed out the horses. "That one's mine." A beautiful bay with one white sock. "His name is Lucky."

"Why Lucky?"

"Because he's lucky to belong to me." He waited for her response and wasn't disappointed. Her eyes sparkled and her lips twitched.

Lucky whinnied and trotted to them. Matt stroked his neck. "You've been out all day. Time for you to rest." They moved on, Lucky following along the fence until he came to a corner and could go no further.

They reached the bunkhouse, and he opened the door. "There's no one here right now."

She peered over his shoulder. "It looks cozy."

He chuckled, amused by her description. "It can get a little rank when there are a dozen hard-working men here."

She backed away. "That's ruined my enjoyment of the place."

The way her eyes crinkled at the corners informed him she wasn't displeased. They moved to the cookhouse. She entered and looked around. Lindy clattered in at Gwen's heels and raced around the big table. Matt opened his mouth to scold her but changed his mind. What harm was she doing? No point in him being grouchy though he preferred to think of it as careful.

A fly buzzed around them, and Gwen waved it away. That reminded him of something he'd heard in town one day. "Why don't cowboys shoo the flies buzzing around?" He asked in an innocent tone.

She swatted at the persistent fly. "Why?"

"It's easier to let them go barefoot."

Her mouth opened and closed. She stared at him. And then the music of her laughter burst free. Guess he'd proved Luke wrong. He hadn't lost his sense of humor. Ma had always found a reason to be happy. He did her memory a disservice if he didn't do the same.

They moved on, sauntering down the trail. "I know so little about you." He was determined to keep the conversation moving along pleasant lines. "What things do you like to do?"

"I'm quite enjoying the evening air. It's so sweet compared to the city. We smell the river and the passing of many men and horses. Here I catch the spicy scent of grass. I can even smell the leaves on the trees." She waved toward the trees along the path. "And birds. So many birds." She paused and tipped her head toward the branches then brought her gaze to him. "I think this might be my new favorite thing to do."

He couldn't think of a single word of response. He couldn't explain why he'd thought she might object to the vast outdoors of the ranch, but he had.

She began walking again. "I also like to read and sew. I'm quite well known for some of my sewing creations."

His thoughts skittered back to seeing Ma bent over a project with needle and thread, the tip of her tongue pressed to her upper lip as she concentrated. Pa had always teased her about how she did that. Lost in memories of days, people, and events that were now gone, he startled when Gwen spoke.

"Tell me what your days look like. I'm imagining you riding across the hills, but I realize you must do more than that," she said.

He chuckled. *See there, Luke, I haven't lost my sense of humor.* "We do ride a lot though some of us have been sticking close to home to watch Lindy."

"Do you mean *you* have?"

She was astute. "It's been mostly me though the others have taken turns." Having Gwen here would free all of them to get back to ranch work.

"What do you do when you're riding?"

"The cows are on open range but unless we keep

them from going too far, they might end up in Canada or lost in the mountains. There's branding, doctoring sick animals, arranging with the neighbors for round-up. There are supplies to buy. We grow oats for feed and we put up hay so that has to be taken care of." He shrugged. "Doesn't sound like much but on a place this size there is always something to do."

The path led past Luke's house and bent toward the valley. They reached a place that allowed them a good view of the blue river below them. The sun rimmed the mountains to the west in pink gold and cast dark shadows across the land. They stood side by side, content to enjoy the scene.

She gasped and caught his arm. "What's that?" She pointed to the bottom of the valley floor.

Lindy stopped running to see what caught Gwen's attention.

A majestic deer dipped his head into the stream of water.

"That's an eight-point buck. He's been hanging around for years. No one on our property will shoot him but I'm surprised other hunters haven't done so. You're fortunate to see him. He doesn't often come out in the open."

"I am blessed." She exhaled softly then turned shining eyes toward him. "Thank you."

He chuckled. "I had nothing to do with it."

She lowered her gaze and then slowly brought it

back to him. "You have everything to do with it. You invited me here."

His mouth went dry as her eyes held his, brown and steady. He licked his lips but couldn't think how to respond.

Lindy raced by, her arms in the air.

She was going fast. They were too close to the edge.

He reached for her, but she slipped from his fingers.

"Lindy, stop," he roared, his heart in his mouth. There was nothing to keep her from plummeting down the side of the hill.

6

*G*wen saw Lindy heading at breakneck speed toward the embankment. One misstep and she'd tumble down the slope. Matt roared for her to stop but she was going too fast and didn't hear him. Gwen reacted out of fear and instinct and leaped forward, putting herself directly in the child's path. Lindy plowed into Gwen, knocking the breath from her. Gwen staggered back a step under the impact.

"Whoa there, little girl." She held Lindy tightly, waiting for her own breathing to settle down and for her heart to stop thumping madly.

Matt caught Lindy's shoulder and pulled her from Gwen. "That was a very foolish thing to do. What if you'd tripped? You'd have—" He shook her. "Don't ever run toward the edge again. Do you hear me?"

Lindy's eyes filled with tears at his harsh tone. "Yes, Uncle Matt."

Matt turned to Gwen. "Are you all right?" He touched her arm.

A sensation like warm sunshine on a spring day spread from where his fingers brushed against her. She nodded. Her throat was so tight it was impossible to get out a word. And then he stepped back taking the warmth with him. It was shock. Nothing more, she told herself and studied the green grass at her feet as her thoughts returned to almost normal. Not that she even knew what normal was at the moment. Everything was new and unfamiliar. New house. New address. New role. New people. Everything.

Except who she was inside. Gwen Humber. But wasn't that soon to change to Gwen Shannon? No wonder she felt off balance.

Matt took Lindy's hand and led them back along the trail toward their house.

The three of them walked in silence. Gwen could feel Matt's displeasure rolling off him like a blast of heat and wasn't sure what to expect. He was understandably upset but how would he handle it? How would he deal with Lindy? The child kept to his side, subdued after his scolding.

He released her. "Lindy, get ready for bed. I'll be back in a few minutes." And he strode away.

Still feeling unsettled, Gwen took Lindy to her

bedroom. "Get your nightgown on and I'll read you a story."

Lindy crumpled up on her bed and started crying. "I didn't mean to be naughty. I was only 'tending to fly."

Gwen shuddered to think where her flying might have landed her. She sat on the bed and pulled the weeping child into her arms. "Both Uncle Matt and I were frightened at how close you were to the edge. We don't want you to get hurt. Promise me you won't pretend to fly when you're anywhere near the valley."

"I won't."

She held the little girl and stroked her hair until she melted against Gwen's chest. Warm and sweet. Gwen kissed the top of her head. "Are you ready to put on your nightie?"

Lindy slipped off Gwen's lap and waited, eyes watching Gwen.

Her throat grew tight with so many emotions—tenderness, gratitude—a myriad of wonderful things. She undid Lindy's buttons and pulled the dress over her head. Smoothed the nightgown as best she could and helped Lindy into it. She'd made sure there was a brush on the nearby dresser and gently brushed the tangled mop.

"Can I braid your hair?" It would be so much tidier in the morning if Lindy allowed it.

Lindy nodded and Gwen trailed her fingers through the locks separating them into strands and enjoying the feel. Even more, she loved the sense of connection between them. She finished and secured the ends with a ribbon tied as tightly as she could. She turned Lindy to face her and kissed her nose. "You look very nice."

Hand in hand they left the room. Gwen wet a cloth and tenderly washed Lindy's face then cleaned her hands enjoying each little finger. They finished as Matt strode into the room.

Gwen felt Lindy tense. She stiffened too, wondering what Matt would do.

He faced them, his expression severe. "Lindy, I've decided something. You are not to go beyond Luke's house. It's too dangerous."

Lindy looked at the floor. Her shoulders rose and fell.

Gwen's heart went out to the child. Certainly, her actions must be corrected but a scolding must make her miss her mother tremendously.

With a slight shudder, Lindy raised her face to Matt. "Yes, Uncle Matt," she said.

"Good. Are you ready for bed?" His tone indicated he was satisfied with her response.

Gwen answered. "I was about to read a story to her." She turned to Lindy. "Do you want Uncle Matt to read too?"

"Like last night?" Lindy's eyes lit up for the first time since she'd crashed into Gwen.

"Is that what you want?"

Her eyes wide, she whispered, "Uh huh."

"Do you know what story you want?"

For an answer, Lindy ran into the bedroom and returned with the book Gwen had brought her. She climbed onto the settee and patted a spot on each side of her.

Gwen met Matt's gaze. Would he be willing? Or was he still upset about the near accident?

Not only did he cross the room and sit beside Lindy, but he looked pleased to do so. They each read the story to Lindy then Gwen took her to bed. Matt asked if he could come but Lindy shook her head.

Gwen listened to her sweet innocent prayer. "God bless"—and she named everyone on the ranch including the cat, her kittens, and the dog. Her voice fell to a whisper as if she didn't want Gwen to hear. "Please help me learn to fly. Amen." She jumped into bed. Gwen pulled the covers to her chin and kissed her on the forehead.

"Sleep tight, little girl." She left the room and rejoined Matt who showed no sign of leaving.

"Would you like tea and another piece of pie?" she asked.

"That'd be great. Thanks." He followed her into the kitchen.

She studied him out of the corner of her eyes as she filled the kettle and prepared the teapot. "You seem troubled." She hoped he wouldn't be offended by her comment, but they couldn't tiptoe around each other if they were to become a family.

"It worries me that Lindy is so wild."

"Was she like that when her parents were alive?"

"I don't remember. It seems whenever I saw her, she was with one of them. They were taking care of her, so I never thought about what she was doing. That was up to them."

"Matt, I think you handled the situation out there very well."

His head came up. His eyes found hers, wide and uncertain. "You do?"

"Yes. She came too close to having an accident." Gwen shuddered. "She needs boundaries. I suppose we all do in some sense."

He quirked his eyebrows. "What sort of boundaries do you have?"

She gave her answer a moment's thought as she set cups of tea on the table for each of them and put a piece of pie before him. She sat down, leaned forward on her elbows, and tried to formulate her words. "Some boundaries are set by God. Like don't steal. Don't lie. Some are set by others. Like say please and thank you. Some we set for ourselves."

"Like what?"

"I told you how my mother said I was her little ray of sunshine. I suppose I wasn't unlike Lindy, happy with life and eager to share my happiness with others. But as I grew older things weren't always easy. Being orphaned and homeless was difficult. I learned things didn't change if I was grumpy but were easier to take if I was happy. Or at least, doing my best to be so. It seemed to make those around me feel better too."

Matt's pie was untouched, his fork forgotten as he listened to her. "Luke accused me of being grouchy." He picked up his fork and poked at the pie.

She kept silent hoping he'd reveal more and ignored her own slice.

"He reminded me of how our mother was always cheerful. I need to be more like her."

Still, Gwen didn't say anything. It seemed to her that he was sorting out his thoughts as he spoke, and she didn't want to interrupt that process.

He sighed heavily. "It's just that there have been so many accidents."

The moments ticked past. Gwen's heart ached at the pain on his face as he sifted through painful memories.

"It wasn't just Roscoe and Merry." He looked up, his dark eyes piercing her like a sword. "You wondered why I didn't meet the train."

She nodded.

"I planned to marry once before."

Ahh, it was as she'd guessed. He'd had his heart broken in the past.

"Corine was her name. I met her when she came to visit her aunt and uncle at the store. We spent every moment I wasn't working together. Shared our thoughts. Laughed at the same things." His throat worked. "We couldn't wait to get married. She went back East to arrange wedding details with her parents then she was to return, and we would marry. I went to meet her on the incoming train. I wished I had a bouquet of hothouse flowers but all I had was a bunch of wildflowers I'd picked. And a little bag of her favorite candy—licorice."

His chest rose and fell steadily as he got caught up in the story. "I sat on the bench outside the depot. The time arrived but no train. After I'd sat there quite some time, Mr. Turner came out. He said there'd been an accident down the line and the train would be delayed. At first, I wasn't concerned. Accidents happen. I was prepared to wait." He paused and she watched his Adam's apple bob as he swallowed.

A heavy feeling settled into her stomach as she guessed what had happened and thought of him waiting, helpless, alone—

"An hour later, Mr. Turner came out again. Telegraph had said there were a number of deaths. I still wasn't concerned. It couldn't mean Corine, and I breathed a little prayer that she wasn't even hurt. Her aunt and uncle had heard the news and came to wait with me. It was dark before the information came that she was one of those who had perished." His hand fisted and he slid it off the table.

Tears gathered in Gwen's throat, making it impossible to speak. She blinked. Forced air into tight lungs.

She clenched her hands tightly, hands that ached to offer comfort with a gentle touch.

"I tossed the wilted flowers to the ground and handed the bag of candy to a child who was among those waiting. It was dark by then, but I rode home at a dangerous pace. I didn't care that it was risky. Life no longer mattered."

He met her eyes, and the depth of his pain stole her breath. "That was the moment my heart died within me. Oh, it pumps blood, but it will never again be alive." He shoved his neglected piece of pie away. "I should have gone with her. But she didn't want to wait until I was free."

With a muffled sound, he strode from the house.

Gwen sat at the table for a long time, digesting his revelation. That explained why he'd insisted on a marriage in name only. Finally, she gathered up the tea service. She'd wash the cups tomorrow. Her steps slow, she went to her bedroom and perched on the edge of her bed.

Their agreement had been for her to be a mother to Lindy. She found utter joy in that. She already loved the child. All she had to do was prove herself to Matt so he would fulfill the promise he'd made to marry her. But now she had another goal. She would do her best to bring joy into Matt's life. She thought of the joke he'd made this afternoon. She liked that side of him.

She opened her Bible and turned to the verse she

had committed to memory when she was young. The words had grown even more encouraging after her parents died and she and Maurice found themselves homeless. *A merry heart doeth good like a medicine: but a broken spirit drieth the bones.* It hadn't always been easy to choose a merry heart, but it always felt better than dwelling on the bad things in her life.

She bent her head and prayed for Lindy and Matt. And that she would be strong.

WANTING to avoid an encounter with anyone or risk having one of his brother's ask what he was doing, Matt headed down the trail away from the buildings. He passed Luke's house. A lamp lit the kitchen, but he didn't see any sign of his brother through the window. Not that he was tempted to go inside and complain about how unsettled things were. He didn't expect or want sympathy.

He scuffed his feet in the dust as he walked. Why had he told Gwen about Corine? He'd only wanted to explain why he hadn't met the train. Somehow, he'd said more than he meant to. He'd never told anyone how shattered he'd been after Corine, though they'd probably been able to tell. He thought of Luke's comment about him being grumpy though he preferred to call it careful. He'd started being so after Corine's death. That was four years ago. The pain had dulled but the habit remained. Reinforced by the accident that claimed Roscoe and his wife's lives. Life was safer if people followed certain rules.

He stared into the darkening sky. He could no longer remember Corine's face. He tried to recall her voice. Instead, he heard a bubble of laughter in his thoughts that he knew to be Gwen's. He groaned. He did not want Gwen to replace Corine in his memories.

His steps slowed as he thought of the time he'd overheard Ma in her bedroom. *Not my will, but thine be done.*

That conscious choice guided her every day through tough times and good times.

Only a faint blush remained in the sky. Matt stopped walking as he considered his own choices. He'd tried to be friendly and amusing when he and Gwen had walked. And it had felt good. He would do his best to continue to do so. Turning, he retraced his steps.

"Howdy, brother." Luke's voice came from the shadows. "Getting dark for a walk."

"Yup."

"Are you having trouble not being grouchy?" He heard the subtle underlying chuckle in his brother's voice.

For a heartbeat, Matt wanted to tell his twin to mind his own business and then realized Luke would already know that's what he was thinking. He laughed. "It can be challenging especially when—"

Luke's voice was soft and somber. "When things are unsettled and changing."

"Yeah." Matt leaned against the house beside Luke. Neither of them spoke for a spell. "Luke, did I ever tell you about seeing Mama cry and go to her bedroom?" He relayed the story to his twin. "Can I do any less than follow her example?"

Luke gave Matt a half-playful punch on the shoulder. "Why'd you never tell me that? I'm your twin. I'm supposed to know everything about you."

"Is that written in a rule book somewhere?" Matt was half annoyed, half amused.

"I expect it is, but we don't need a rule book. We just know each other."

Matt didn't argue because it was true. He waited, understanding Luke had something more on his mind.

"Matt, I know it's been hard for you in many ways. Losing Corine just before your wedding was horrible." He bumped his shoulder into Matt's. "We have to move on. Ma and Pa would want it. I think Corine would want it. Roscoe and Merry would too."

"I know, but it's not easy."

"I think your Gwen has been sent to help us on that journey. Wally said he heard her and Lindy laughing together and watched them walking down the trail, holding hands. You know I was joshing about taking your place when she came, but I've come to the conclusion she's just what that little girl needs, and I think she might be just what you need too."

"Me?" He was about to deny that he needed anything but what was the point? Luke would believe he was right because he thought he knew Matt better than Matt knew himself. He longed to rush away but if he did Luke would figure it was because he didn't care to hear the truth. Instead, he changed the subject. "Has Riley gone to his house?" He told Luke about Gwen's thoughts that she might be coming to a tar paper shack.

Luke chuckled. "And yet she came. Brave girl."

Yeah. Guess she is.

"And then you didn't marry her. I'm surprised she didn't turn around and get back on that train."

"It's just a delay." Although he might not feel as strongly about it as he once had.

Luke shifted. Matt braced himself for another punch on the shoulder, but Luke only rearranged himself.

"What exactly are you uncertain about? Are you hoping to fall in love with her?"

Disgusted with Luke's foolishness, Matt strode away. "I'm going to see what Andy's doing."

"You can't outrun your thoughts," Luke called.

He wasn't trying to outrun anything. He entered the silent house. The last couple of months they'd all gathered in the kitchen. Lindy raced about until bedtime. Before that, Roscoe and Merry had always been around. At one time, Pa's presence had filled the place. Matt grinned. Pa always seemed larger than life.

And long ago, Ma had been there, her quiet, sweet spirit offering calm to any situation.

Matt sighed. A lonely sound he was grateful no one heard. He peeked into the sitting room where they gathered in the winter months. Though he wondered if they would do so again. They each had their own homes. He would have Gwen and Lindy in his. The others had no one. He'd suggest they should be trying to find wives too. Amusement tickled his insides at the idea of doing so.

His gaze went to the chair where Ma would sit and then to the one where Pa had spent the evenings. Sometimes the boys had been there playing games or reading. Even after they built their own houses, they preferred this place. Guess he could understand why Lindy balked at leaving the only home she'd ever known. Gwen was wise to recognize the child needed time to adjust.

His gaze settled on the bookshelf near Ma's chair. Was that her Bible? He crossed the room and pulled the book out. It was, indeed. He flipped the pages until he found the picture of the angel. It was as he remembered. The same as the one in Lindy's book.

He sat on the floor, the Bible open on his legs, when footsteps sounded behind him.

"Hi, Andy. I thought you were in bed."

"It's too quiet. I'm glad you're here."

He turned back to the Bible. "I think I'll borrow this and read it if no one objects."

Andy snorted. "Only one here to do so is me and I don't see any reason you can't borrow it."

Matt didn't miss the emphasis on borrow.

"Why do you want it?" Andy asked.

He showed the illustration to Andy and explained about the book Gwen had given to Lindy.

His younger brother dropped into Ma's chair. "You think it means something? That it has the same picture?"

Maybe that thought had crossed Matt's mind, but he wasn't about to admit it. "I think it means it's a frequently-used illustration. Nothing more."

Andy leaned forward. "What do you think of her?"

"Who?" As if Andy could mean anyone but Gwen.

Andy jabbed Matt's leg with his toe. "You know who I mean."

"I'm guessing Gwen. She's all right as far as I can tell." He itemized mentally what he knew about her. She could cook. She liked to laugh. She didn't mind having an opinion that differed from his and letting him know. That could make life uncomfortable in the future. "I'm not about to jump into something permanent without being sure."

"Then why'd you ask her to come? Doesn't seem right."

He wasn't about to admit to his younger brother that he hadn't allowed doubts until he was on his way to town. Andy would laugh and say it sounded like a typical groom's cold feet. "I gave her a chance to say she didn't agree to waiting a month." But why he'd asked her to make the decision wasn't as easy to put into words. "Guess I want to make sure she was right for Lindy." Not even to himself would he admit he was now wondering if she was a good fit for *him* because that was not part of his plan. Like he'd told Gwen, he'd loved once and had the wounds on his heart.

"Well so long as you aren't wishing she was Corine."

Matt closed the Bible slowly and pushed to his feet.

Why was everyone—himself included—suddenly thinking of Corine? That was the past and he'd moved on.

But was it truly past and forgotten? Would it ever be?

7

*G*wen had decided she must say something about Matt's confession last night. She didn't want him to think she wasn't sympathetic toward his loss. She'd even shed a few tears into her pillow as she thought of his pain. Not that he needed to know that.

She had breakfast ready when he came to the house. Lindy had set the table. Knowing how much Matt liked everything in place, Gwen had gone around quickly and straightened the cutlery when Lindy wasn't watching.

Her heart lightened when Matt entered, smiling and greeting them with a cheery, "Good morning."

"Good morning to you," she replied. At least he wasn't grumpy as Luke had accused him. "I made my special breakfast cake today." She'd also made savory pancakes that she guessed were not part of his usual fare. If he didn't like them, she wouldn't make them again.

"Cake?" He blinked. One eyebrow quirked and then he smiled. "Why not?"

"Lindy's excited about the idea. It's cinnamon coffee cake. My mother taught me to make it."

"Then I assume it is very special."

She beamed. "It's also very delicious." His acknowlegment meant far more than he would ever know.

He washed his hands and took his place at the table. Lindy was already seated and waiting.

"Aunt Gwen let me lick the bowl but said I had to wait until you got here to taste anything more." Lindy squirmed. "I never had breakfast cake before."

"I haven't either. Pa always insisted there must be eggs and meat and potatoes at breakfast. He allowed pancakes or fresh biscuits as well. Nothing different though. Guess we all just followed his orders. Though I can't think why we continue to do so." He chuckled.

A sound that settled into the pit of Gwen's stomach like a warm, sweet drink. The man ought to laugh more. It suited him.

"Hurry and pray, Uncle Matt." Lindy's gaze was riveted to the cake Gwen had put in the middle of the table, alongside a bowl of boiled eggs—did Matt prefer them always fried?

After he'd said grace, she offered him the platter holding the savory potato pancakes and explained, "They don't need syrup though my father liked applesauce on his. Try them and if you don't like them, I won't make them again."

He took a cautious bite while she waited. His eyes widened but she couldn't tell if it was in enjoyment or dislike. He swallowed. "Gwen, that is the best thing I've ever had for breakfast."

"I'm glad." Pleasure made her blink twice.

Lindy ate one pancake and an egg. But her gaze lingered on the coffee cake. She wiped her plate clean. "I'm done."

Although he'd eaten much more, Matt finished seconds after Lindy. His gaze also went to the cake and then he raised his eyes to look at Gwen.

Laughter rippled across her lips. "Look at the two of you."

Matt shifted his attention to Lindy and chuckled. "We've never had cake for breakfast."

"I hope I haven't built up unreasonable expectations." She slid a large square to Matt's plate and a smaller one to Lindy's then sat back to await their verdict.

Lindy ate a mouthful. "It's good." She didn't even raise her gaze from her plate.

Matt lifted a forkful to his mouth and chewed. He grinned, making his eyes crinkle at the edges. "It's delicious." He glanced at the serving bowls and the empty platter. "I do believe this is the best breakfast I've ever had. Thank you."

Happiness bubbled inside Gwen. She'd impressed

him. They finished the meal and Matt excused Lindy from the table. She ran outside to play, leaving the house quiet. Matt seemed content to linger over a second cup of coffee. Gwen could think of no reason why she shouldn't remain as well and pulled her cup closer even though it was empty.

"Matt, I didn't get a chance to express my feelings last night after you told me about Corine. Let me say that although I can't begin to understand the shock of learning of her death, I am truly sorry for your loss. It's obvious you were very much in love." She'd never known that sort of love and knew she never would. The few times she'd had a beau seemed such a pale comparison to his feelings.

He studied the contents of his cup and then slowly lifted his head to look at her. "It was four years ago."

"Something as earth-shattering as that isn't easily forgotten. I believe it shapes our lives in ways we can't comprehend."

His gaze returned to the cup cradled between his palms. "Thanks for your understanding." He downed his coffee in three gulps and pushed from the table. "Time for me to get to work. Thanks for breakfast." With that, he was gone.

Gwen remained at the table. Understanding? Did she want that? But what else was there? She refused to acknowledge the hollowness pressing at her heart, tightening her throat.

Enough pining over what could not be hers.

She stored away the food, gathered up the dishes, washed them, and put everything back on the shelves. From the kitchen window, she glimpsed Lindy flitting back and forth and smiled. Gwen could create tasty meals and be a mother to the child. She did not want more. She did not long for a love that filled her heart and life to overflowing.

Scolding herself for useless thoughts, she turned to study the kitchen. There were no cookies in the house. She meant to correct that immediately and pulled out mixing bowls and baking sheets. Soon the kitchen held the sweet spicy scent of ginger cookies.

The outer door opened, surprising her. She expected the aroma had carried outside and drawn Lindy in. But the footsteps were too heavy to be a child's. Matt entered.

"We have visitors. Thought I should warn you."

"Visitors? And just in time for fresh cookies. Help yourself." She indicated the cooling rack. "Where are they?"

"Coming down the trail. They'll be here in ten minutes or so."

"Perfect. That's all the time I need to finish cleaning up." She'd already washed the mixing bowls and quickly scoured the last baking tray. She put away everything and spread a clean tablecloth on the table. Too bad she didn't have something to put in the center to brighten the place. She glanced around. She'd hung a few pictures, but the house needed more decorating.

Matt stood in the kitchen eating his third or fourth cookie.

She studied him. "Do they pass inspection?"

He grinned. "They sure do. Gwen, you're a fine cook."

"Thank you." At the sound of an approaching wagon, she whipped off her apron and hung it behind the stove. She smoothed her skirt and ran her hands over her hair

Matt watched her. "You look fine. Just fine."

Her cheeks warmed at his approval and then she went to the door with him to greet their visitors. A young couple with two children—a boy, Gwen guessed to be about Lindy's age and a girl maybe a year or two older.

"It's the Dixons," Matt murmured close to her ear. "They live to the north about ten miles." He introduced Gwen to Mrs. Dixon.

"Please call me Opal. We're your nearest neighbors so no need for formality."

"Her husband, Vern Dixon." Gwen heard the amusement in Matt's voice.

Opal indicated her children. "Sarah and Junior."

Gwen welcomed them into the house. For a moment, she wondered if she should show them to the sitting room but before she could make up her mind, Opal told Vern to get something out of the wagon. He returned with a large pot holding a flowering rose.

"I've kept it inside all winter that's why it has so

many blooms," Opal explained. "You can keep it indoors or plant it somewhere. Whatever you like. It's my way of saying welcome to your new home. I hope you'll be very happy."

"Thank you." Gwen took the gift and dipped her head into the roses. "They smell so good."

"Not near as good as those cookies," Mr. Dixon said, eyeing the cooling rack.

"Vern," his wife scolded.

Laughing, Gwen waved them in. "Please join us for fresh cookies and tea…unless you prefer coffee?"

"Tea is fine," Opal said. "Where's Lindy?"

Matt stepped outside and called her. She eased from the bushes. "Come on, Lindy. It's the Dixons that come for tea. You know them. Sarah and Junior are here to play."

Gwen wanted to linger and see what Lindy was going to do but her guests required her attention. Mr. Dixon pulled out a chair and sat down, solving Gwen's questions as to whether they should go to the sitting room. Matt and Lindy joined them though Lindy seemed reluctant.

Gwen thought she would be glad for the company, especially as Matt indicated she knew them. Matt got a bench from outdoors and put it along one side of the table for the children to sit on. The adults used the chairs

Mr. Dixon directed his question to Matt. "How does the grass look where your cows are?"

"It's not growing the way it should this time of year."

"Sure could use a rain." Mr. Dixon took the cup of tea Gwen offered him and helped himself to two cookies.

The children each took one. All three of them shifted on the bench, as uneasy as if they were in church.

Gwen looked at Opal. "Would you be offended if the children took their cookies and went to play?"

"That's a good idea. Run along." She shooed them toward the door.

The two Dixon children raced away. Lindy finished her cookie before she left the house.

Gwen watched her go, wondering if she felt strange around the other children. The child was used to being with grown-ups. Her only playmates were the dog and cats. She glanced out the window to see Lindy racing after Junior. Satisfied the little girl was happy playing with the others, she turned her attention back to the adults.

Mr. Dixon drained his cup, took two more cookies, and pushed his chair back. "Matt, let's go look at your horses and leave these women to have a chin wag."

Matt looked at Gwen. As if asking her if she was all right with him leaving. Knowing he cared, that spot deep within again made its presence known. She smiled. "That sounds nice."

As soon as the men departed, Opal leaned forward.

"Merry and Roscoe were dear friends. It was such a tragedy the way they died. And poor Lindy. But at least she had the Shannons to provide her a home and now she has you. I must say I was delighted to hear that the girl would get a mother. Now tell me about yourself."

Gwen laughed softly and Opal laughed too. "You'll have to forgive me. But I don't see near enough of other people and Vern and I run out of things to say to each other. Where are you from?"

Gwen told of growing up in a small city along the Mississippi River. "My father oversaw shipping along the river until his passing. What about you? Where are you from?"

Opal had been born and raised near Fort Benton. "So I'm familiar with river traffic." She told Gwen many things about the Crow Crossing area, the ranchers, and their wives.

"The women get together from time to time for a quilting bee. You might enjoy that." Opal said.

"I most certainly would. I love sewing."

"Me too, though my time is mostly used in making clothes for two growing children."

Gwen hesitated a moment before she spoke again. "I make clothes, of course. I've made quilts. I brought one with me." The others she'd left behind but wondered if Patricia would throw them out simply because Gwen had made them. "But what I love doing most is creating special dolls for children."

"Rag dolls. That's nice."

They weren't ordinary rag dolls but not knowing how they would be received, Gwen wasn't ready to show her creations to anyone just yet.

Mr. Dixon came back at that moment. "We need to be on our way. Thank you for everything." They rounded up their children and returned to the wagon.

"Nice to meet you," Opal called. "Welcome to our part of the world, Mrs. Shannon."

"I'm not—" But her words were drowned out by the rattle of the wagon. "I'm not Mrs. Shannon," she finished softly with only Matt to hear her.

MATT WATCHED Gwen's expression grow wary. Then she smiled. "I guess they'll learn the truth soon enough, but I don't want them to think I was trying to deceive them."

No doubt everyone in the community was aware that he'd been expecting a mail-order bride. He didn't care if they knew, any more than he cared whether or not they approved.

But her concerns were valid. They'd expect he had married her. His reasons for his sudden change of heart on the way to town no longer seemed quite so compelling "I've put you in an awkward position. I'm sorry."

"You didn't force me to agree. The Dixons seem like nice people."

He gladly turned to other things. "They are. They moved in here a few years ago. He and some other investors purchased the lease. Vern is a good operator. He and Pa were among the few that survived the bad winter of '86-'87 with minimal losses. Pa prepared for such a winter." Matt grinned. "An old native friend had warned him to expect a bad one. He'd put up hay and told Vern to do the same. He warned the others, but they didn't pay him any mind. We moved our cattle to lower pastures before the snow hit. Vern followed our example."

"I can see you're proud of that accomplishment and you should be."

"Pa was a wise man. I hope we are as good. I figure it takes all four of us working together to have the know-how of our father."

She laughed at his assessment. "I'm sorry I didn't get to meet him. Or your mother."

"They would have liked you." He hadn't given his words any thought before uttering them, but he knew them to be true. And it surprised him.

Her eyes gleaming, she pressed her fingers to his forearm. "Thank you for saying so. It means more to me than you can guess."

It was not the first time she'd touched him. Was she even aware that she did so or was she only reaching out to him like she would have to Lindy? He'd ignore it. Pretend the feel of her fingers didn't have the ability to travel along his veins and reach into the depths of his heart to nestle there, carrying promise. He'd pretend he wasn't aware of her so close, that he didn't inhale something as sweet as spring flowers.

But those feelings did not go along with his decision, and he stiffened.

Her gaze darted away and then returned before he could even miss it. And time ticked by in solitary seconds. He heard nothing but the beat of his heart. Saw nothing but the surprise—and dare he believe? — hope in her eyes. A vast universe of possibility.

She lowered her head and withdrew her hand. At the same time, he stepped back so they no longer touched. He had no idea what had just happened. Or if anything had. Perhaps he was suffering from some kind of spring fever. *When a young man's fancy lightly turns to thoughts of love.*

Where had he heard that? Likely from Luke and as such, he dismissed it. He had no time or room in his life for silliness. Romance was for children and the unwary. He was neither. Nor did he wish to repeat painful lessons of the past.

"Luke and I are riding to the northwest to check on the water supply. The others are taking goods to the line shacks." Even Wally, he realized. "You'll be alone." Maybe he should tell Luke he'd have to go without him.

"I'll be fine. You go about your work and don't worry about me."

"Are you sure?"

"Matt, what would your father expect of you?"

"I admired my father. He was a wise rancher. But he wasn't the wisest husband. I don't want to be like him in that regard."

Something shifted in Gwen's expression. She grew thoughtful. He was tempted to say yearning filled her eyes. Obviously, he was muddled from thinking of his parents.

"I'll be fine. You go riding with Luke. Enjoy the day. Lindy and I are going to keep busy."

That piqued his curiosity. "What do you have planned?" Should he stay behind and make sure they didn't encounter problems?

Her eyes twinkled as if she knew what he was thinking. "We're going to check out the garden. Maybe pick flowers. Nothing of importance. I simply want to spend time with the child."

Nothing he was needed for. Not that he was disappointed. "Well, enjoy your day."

"You too," she called as he strode away.

It might be fun to spend the day with Lindy and Gwen. But he had work to do and wasn't part of his reason for asking Gwen to come to free up the men to do their work?

Luke greeted him in the barn. They saddled their

horses and rode from the yard. "I can see you're thrilled with my company."

Matt smiled though it didn't do much but lift the corners of his mouth.

Luke continued, not bothered by Matt's lack of response. "You know everyone would understand if you stayed behind. This is the month you're supposed to be getting to know Gwen. Can't do that if you're out riding the range."

"Let's go check that draw." He urged his horse forward. But Luke made a valid point.

How was he to get to know Gwen if he didn't spend time with her? Never mind the evenings together. Or the morning he'd spent having tea with her and the Dixons. The latter certainly didn't count.

Could he find a way to be with her more? Did he want to?

8

*G*wen checked her hair in the glass one last time. It was neatly coiled around her head. Lindy was in a clean dress, her twin braids tied with ribbon.

"We're ready," Gwen announced.

Matt had informed them last night that he needed to make a trip to Crow Crossing to get supplies. When he asked if she'd like to accompany him, her answer had come eagerly.

"I'd love to. I saw little of the town when I arrived."

"That's my fault." He rubbed at the back of his neck. "I should have realized we needed a delay before you started your journey." His mouth pulled down. "That was an oversight on my part."

She'd chuckled and patted his hand... something she wanted to do more often than she could find reason for. "I'm not blaming you, circumstances being what they were."

"Still, I should have given it more thought."

She wasn't sure if he meant the trip from town, or his decision to put off the wedding and hoped was the latter. Last night, she'd posed the question, "Do I need to prepare anything? A lunch?"

"Make a list of things you need to buy." He paused then added, "Lunch would be nice."

Lindy bounced up and down at the prospect of the trip. Gwen contained her excitement to soft laughter at the child's enthusiasm.

Lindy stood still long enough to ask, "Can I get a candy stick?"

Gwen had a few dollars and could buy the child a treat but before she could answer, Lindy bounced across the room. "I'll ask Uncle Matt. He'll say yes."

Seeing Lindy so confident in Matt's generosity boosted Gwen's opinion of the man. She laughed softly. Despite her initial disappointment at his delay of the wedding, he'd been slowly, but steadily, climbing in her esteem.

A basket held the simple lunch she'd prepared. There were cold potato pancakes, boiled eggs, chunks of cheese, and dill pickles from a crock she'd found in the pantry. She'd made a raisin loaf she thought Matt would enjoy and baked cookies. She might have done more but there hadn't been time.

The wagon rumbled to the house, and she heard

the brake squeak into place. She tied her bonnet on as Matt stepped inside.

"Everyone ready?" he asked.

Lindy raced for the door without answering. Matt jumped out of her way as she tore past. He looked at Gwen. A feeling as strange and yet familiar as her dreams rushed up her throat at the way his smile started at the corners of his mouth and moved upward in one swift movement to fill his eyes so they glistened. She'd never before understood that description but now she did.

A deep sound broke the silence that had engulfed her. He was laughing. A bubble of answering amusement raced up her throat and past her lips. She'd learned to laugh and enjoy life, thanks in large part to her mother's encouragement, but this felt entirely different. It was as if he'd poured the feeling into her. Her gaze locked with his.

His smile softened. "Are you ready?"

His words broke the spell. She shifted her gaze away, trying to make sense of her thoughts and indicated the basket. "Our lunch."

He took the container and waved her ahead of him out the door. Matt set the basket in the back of the wagon where Lindy waited and then held out a hand to assist Gwen to the seat.

She rested her palm in his and almost gasped at the way her nerves jolted at the touch. She swallowed hard. What was wrong with her?

Her insides calmed as Matt made his way around the horses and up to the seat beside her and drove from the yard. Unsettled by her unexpected reactions, she concentrated on the landscape as they journeyed along the trail.

"Have you ever driven a wagon?"

She laughed at the absurdity of his question. She'd lived in town where she could walk most places and if her destination was too far, she asked Maurice to take her or hired a driver. "I have not."

"Then it's time you learned."

She stared at him. Never mind the twinkle in his eyes. "I don't wish to drive a wagon."

"You'll need to know if you want to visit Opal or go to town on your own."

She couldn't argue with that, but she'd never had any desire to be in control of two large horses. The thin pieces of leather seemed inadequate for the task.

"Here, take the reins."

She shook her head. His eyes narrowed for a second then he smiled—a beguiling smile if she'd ever seen one. Completely ignoring her resistance, he placed the reins in her hands.

"You hold them this way. To turn them you pull this way or that." He moved her hands, and the horses began to leave the road. He moved her hands the other way and they returned. "To stop, you pull back but for now, the trail is straight, and the horses know what to do."

He leaned away, leaving her with narrow strips of leather in her hands and her heart in her mouth. "Matt!"

"You can do this. Relax."

She tried to, but the feeling was oddly like running down a hill faster than she should be able to.

"Doesn't it feel good?"

She laughed, a sound more nervous than amused. "I'm driving the wagon."

"Yes, you are."

Lindy leaned over the bench. "Can I learn?"

Matt chuckled. "When you're older." The sound filled Gwen with an emotion as unfamiliar as the reins in her hands. She sought for a way to describe it. A name to give it. But nothing came to mind. She'd simply have to enjoy it.

They rolled on, the horses needing no guidance from Gwen, and she began to relax. Matt was beside her. The day was lovely. Lindy had stopped bouncing around and sat in the back of the wagon. All was right in her world. She was almost ready to thank Patricia for forcing this move on her.

A shadow erupted from the trees beside the trail. The horses broke into a gallop. Gwen jolted, her heart hammering with alarm. The wagon bounced, practically throwing her from the seat. She gripped the reins but didn't know what else to do.

"Matt!"

His hands closed around hers. "I've got this. Let me take the reins."

The calmness of his voice enabled her to suck in air. Slowly, she withdrew her fingers. Matt pulled back, calling to the horses to whoa.

The wagon bounced and lurched. Gwen held to the seat to keep from being thrown out. Her throat closed off. She sucked in her lips and prayed that Lindy was safe in the back.

They slowed and came to a halt, the horses breathing loudly. Matt sat back. Sweat beaded his forehead. They stared at each other, fear still claiming her. Nausea made her dizzy. She should have never let him convince her to try controlling the wagon. She had no idea what to do to stop the horses. They could have all been killed.

Tears she never allowed burned her eyes.

Matt set the brake. He looked back to check on Lindy. She held to the side of the wagon, her eyes big.

"That was scary." Then she laughed. "And fun."

Seeing she was all right, Matt turned to Gwen, her shoulder softly shaking with sobs. His heart twisted with something different than the panic that had claimed him a few minutes ago. Not knowing what else to do and acting out of an instinct he hadn't been aware of, he pulled her to his chest. "We're safe. No harm done."

She clutched his shirt front. "It's my fault. I didn't know what to do." Each word came out on a sob.

If anyone could be blamed, it was Matt. Thinking about how this might have turned out, his arms tightened around her. Was this how Roscoe and Merry had ended? Their hearts screaming with fear before they crashed. Did Lindy realize the similarity to her parents' accident? He glanced back again but her attention was on the trail behind them.

"Uncle Matt, look."

A cow moose trotted away, two calves at her heels.

He eased Gwen up. "That's what frightened the horses." He pointed, trying to divert her attention from her fear.

She dried her eyes on her sleeve so she could see.

"We came between the cow and her babies. She was protecting them."

Gwen sniffled. "Good for her but what a scare." She tipped her head to look into Matt's face.

His eyes followed the trail of dampness on her cheeks, remnants of her tears. His gaze stopped at her eyes, full of...what? Gratitude at being alive, he supposed, though it felt more personal, more intimate than that.

Death could have so easily claimed her. He hadn't forgotten how much it hurt to lose someone he cared for. *Stop right there.* He would not be going in that direction. Thankfully, he hadn't let himself grow fond of her. Heat rose behind his eyeballs as he insisted that was the truth. "We best be on our way." He eased her from his arms, took up the reins, and continued the journey.

Everyone was quiet for the remainder of the trip until town came into sight. He'd promised to show Gwen around and he turned down the first side street. They passed half a dozen houses before he pulled to a halt in front of the church.

"Crow Crossing Church," he announced. "We'll go tomorrow morning. It's one of the earliest buildings apart from the businesses on Main Street. Thanks to Ma. She insisted we must have a church. She persuaded Pa to donate money and then visited the other ranchers to convince them the area would benefit from having a place of worship. Within a year of our arrival, this building was erected. We had an older man as preacher at first, but he passed on one winter and Reverend Ingram and his wife replaced him. They have a daughter, Edie, but she hasn't been here for a long time."

"Where is she?"

"Gone east as far as I know."

Gwen's attention went to the graveyard beside the church. She gave him a look full of silent questioning.

He lowered his voice. "My parents are there. So are hers." He tipped his head to indicate he meant Lindy.

He urged the horses forward and returned to Main Street.

Gwen looked from side to side, taking in all the businesses, not that there were many—the blacksmith shop, a harness shop, and the mercantile where he pulled to a halt. Beyond that was the livery barn and across the street, the railway station.

Lindy was on the ground immediately. "Uncle Matt, can I have a candy stick?"

"Yes, you may." He alighted and reached up to assist Gwen. He said, "Buy anything you need. Mr. Luckham will put it on my bill." Taking her elbow, he guided her into the store.

Both Mr. and Mrs. Luckham were there and no other customers. The older couple looked up at his entrance and immediately crossed the store toward them.

"Welcome, welcome," Mrs. Luckham said.

"Mr. and Mrs. Luckham, I'd like you to meet Miss Gwen Humber."

"Miss?" Shock thinned the woman's words.

"We haven't been to the preacher yet."

Mrs. Luckham gave him a look of disapproval. "Why not?" She tsked. "It's time you moved on. Put the past behind you."

She looked about to say more. Mrs. Luckham was known as a source of news...or a busybody, depending on how you viewed it. Matt guessed she was about to blurt out something about Corine. He didn't intend to give her the opportunity and spoke through his clenched teeth.

"Miss Humber will pick out what she wants. Lindy can have a candy stick. Here's a list of supplies for the ranch. I'll be back later for them." He was out of the store before anyone could say jack rabbit. The wagon tipped as he climbed aboard and drove down the street, passing the livery and the train depot, his attention focused toward the front until the town lay behind him. He was dizzy and realized he'd forgotten to breathe.

Pulling to a halt, he stared into the distance. Why did he let Mrs. Luckham bother him? Or was he upset because she reminded him of the times he'd spent with Corine, often calling at the store to take her for an outing? His insides twisted and turned like a prairie whirlwind. He stared straight ahead until his breathing grew normal and the feelings triggered by Mrs. Luckham's comments had vanished.

Poor Gwen. She must wonder if he'd abandoned her. He turned around and made his way back to town. He approached the train station. His gaze went in that direction and stayed there as the wagon rolled by. He had not mounted the steps to the platform since Corine's death. But why did he let it guide his decisions now? He pulled to a halt in front of the store and sat a moment. Marrying Gwen was different than his plans to marry Corine. It was only for Lindy's sake. So why this churning inside?

Only because he had been neglectful toward Gwen. And he meant to make up for it starting right now with the plans he'd made for the day.

He strode into the store. Gwen met his gaze. He smiled and was rewarded with the answering brightness on her face. Her eyes were soft and welcoming. A box and sacks full of beans, rice, and cornmeal stood on the counter.

"Your order is ready," Mr. Luckham said.

"Thanks. Are you done with your shopping?" He directed the question to Gwen.

She nodded and for some reason, he couldn't tear his gaze from her.

Mrs. Luckham chuckled, and he jerked his attention toward her. "I've enjoyed getting to know Gwen. I believe the two of you will make a perfect couple."

It wasn't that sort of arrangement. But he kept his words to himself. No one else needed to know the circumstances of their agreement. He loaded the supplies and then helped Gwen to the seat. Lindy, sucking on a red-and-white candy stick, jumped into the back on her own.

He thanked the Luckhams and drove away. "I'm sorry for leaving you there on your own."

"Matt, I am capable of shopping without assistance. Mrs. Luckham was very helpful."

I'm sure she was. "Did she tell you about everyone in the area?"

She laughed softly. "Well, let me see. If I'm to

believe everything she says there are a dozen or more cowboys in the area who would be glad to have a pretty young thing like me arrive in town, ready and willing to get married." She laughed. "I looked around to see if she meant me."

"Who else would she mean?"

"I'm neither pretty nor young but if it pleases her to say so, I'll not correct her."

"My ma said a person should receive compliments with a gracious thank you." Matt might have wondered if Gwen was fishing for a compliment, but her soft chuckle suggested she was teasing.

"Oh, believe me, I expressed my thanks." Her eyes brimmed with amusement, trapping him in a web of pleasure.

She continued. "She said I must attend the next quilting bee. She'll let me know on Sunday when it's to be." Gwen's voice was round with hidden laughter. "When I said I didn't see how I could, she patted my arm like I was missing something and said, of course, I would." She chuckled. "I'm guessing Mrs. Luckham is used to having her *suggestions* followed."

At the apt observation regarding the storekeeper's wife, Matt laughed. "I'll be sure you are able to attend, or she'll be after my hide."

Their gazes caught and held in shared amusement. She was the first to look away. "Where are we going?"

While they talked, he'd been guiding the wagon away from town but in the opposite direction of the ranch. "I thought you'd like to eat before we return home." How easy it was to say home and mean it for her as well as himself and Lindy.

She looked around. "Are you taking me to a special place?"

Special? He hadn't thought of it that way. It was a spot he and Corine had enjoyed. Shouldn't he be wanting to keep the place just between Corine and himself? He shrugged. "It's an often-used place by the river. Many go there for picnics." And courting. But this time he was only going for the former. He turned off the road to a grassy trail. With a jolt, he realized the last time he'd been here was with Corine before she'd gone home to make arrangements for their wedding.

His attention shifted to more immediate concerns as he guided the wagon between trees and around rocks until they reached the grassy bank of the river where he stopped.

Lindy jumped down, but Gwen and Matt sat taking in the scene. This side of the river was a gentle, treed slope except for a high spot to the right. The far side had a steep, rocky bank. His gaze went toward a thicket of trees to the left. He and Corine had put their blanket there and spent the afternoon making plans. He'd kissed her tenderly knowing she was leaving on the morning train, and he wouldn't see her for several weeks.

He'd never seen her again.

He must have groaned or sighed overly loud because Gwen touched his arm. "Is something wrong?"

Matt looked away from that spot. "No." He got down and reached up to help her.

Her feet on the ground, she looked into his face. "I feel there is something about this place that bothers you. Do you want to change your mind and go elsewhere?" Her eyes were so gentle and kind that he decided he wanted nothing more than to provide her a time of enjoyment.

He put his memories aside and smiled down at her. "I can think of no place I'd sooner have a picnic." Her flashing smile brought an echoing happiness to his heart.

"Then let's have a picnic."

The air was suddenly clearer as he reached for the basket of food and the quilt he'd tossed in.

"Wait. Let's explore first, if you don't mind." Gwen looked almost as eager as Lindy who raced up and down the trail, her arms flapping.

"Let's." He left the supplies in the wagon and together they walked along the bank.

"It's such a cheerful little stream compared to what I'm used to."

Of course. Kellom was along the Mississippi. This river must look unremarkable in contrast.

She continued. "It seems to sing as it hurries along. And it's so clear. I can see the rocks at the bottom."

"It will run fuller when the snow melts on the mountains."

"What's the name of this river?"

"Well, if Pa had his way, it would be called Shannon River." His expression and tone were serious.

She grinned widely. "But it's not?"

"It's Crow River."

"Ahh, so that's why the town is Crow Crossing?"

"Pa objected to that as well."

"Lindy talks about her crow family."

"Birds?" he asked.

She gave him a curious look. "Yes. What else would it be?"

"Crow Crossing refers to a native tribe. It seems it was a common place for them to cross. Back when..."

"When what?" she prodded.

"When they were free to roam and hunt buffalo." He heard the deepening of his voice as he thought of those former days.

They stood in contemplative silence for a moment then resumed their walk. Gwen expressed pleasure at everything they saw—ducks swimming on the water with little ducklings in their wake, tiny white flowers hiding behind rocks, and the different leaves on different trees. He was pleased to be able to provide the names of the trees but couldn't identify the white flower.

They entered a grove of willows. Lindy dashed from one tree to the next. She skidded to a halt in front of them. "I'm hungry. Can I please have some-thing to eat?"

Gwen looked at Matt. "Picnic time?"

They retraced their steps to the wagon. The lunch was soon set out and they sat on the quilt in the long, soft grass. Tossing aside his hat, he said grace then leaned back on one elbow as he partook of the food Gwen had prepared. He liked her cooking.

He realized he also enjoyed her company.

Well, what was wrong with that? If they were to marry there should be peace and pleasure between them. They finished the meal, entertained by Lindy's chatter. He made no move to gather up the quilt and basket, nor return to the wagon.

He pushed himself upright. "Would you like to explore the other direction?"

"If you aren't in a hurry to get home." She slowly packed away the remnants of food.

"No need to rush back." He pulled her to her feet. Reluctantly, he released her hand. And mentally kicked himself for such foolishness. There was no room for a wish for touching and holding in their agreement. His thoughts back where they belonged, he walked beside her.

They wandered along the edge of the water following Lindy as she ran along the bluff six feet above them, her arms out like a bird.

The grassy area narrowed making it necessary for them to walk closer to the water.

"Aunt Gwen, look at me." Lindy flapped her arms.

"Be careful," he called.

"I can fly."

"Don't!" His warning was too late. His heart fisted into his ribs as Lindy launched herself off the bank. Acting out of sheer instinct he lunged forward, almost tripping over Gwen. His fingers closed over Lindy's dress, and he jerked back to keep her from hitting the ground. Spray dampened him as Lindy's hands skimmed the water. He set the uninjured child on her feet. She wiped the water from her face.

"Don't ever do that again." The words were loud and sharp, but he couldn't help it. His heart still pounded with urgency.

Wriggling free of his grasp, she raced into the trees.

He turned back to Gwen. At the sight of her sitting in the river, the icy water up to her waist, his breath stalled.

"I knocked you over." It was half question, half statement and all regret making it difficult to get his words out clearly. He pulled her to her feet.

"A little water never hurt anyone." Her teeth chattered.

"You might have been hurt. As it is, you might take a chill." He hustled her back to the wagon and wrapped the quilt around her, keeping her in his arms.

Should he start a fire or hurry home? It would take almost an hour to reach the ranch.

"Sit here." He left her on the dry grass and gathered

wood and kindling. He soon had a fire blazing. What if she caught pneumonia from this incident? He couldn't blame Lindy. He should have been watching her more closely. He should have been more careful. His stomach knotted. His fists clenched. The helpless feeling of being unable to prevent bad things from happening clawed at his throat.

"You saved Lindy from a nasty fall." Gwen touched his arm. "But I think she got wet."

He covered Gwen's icy hand with his. Frustration and concern mounted inside. "Her behavior is unacceptable."

"Be easy on her. She's just a child and meant no harm."

Gwen's gentle words settled some of the churning in his stomach. "Lindy," he called. But the child did not come running as usual. He stood and turned full circle. He called again. Still nothing.

Couldn't he keep track of one four-year-old? And keep a grown woman safe?

A familiar burning filled the inside of his stomach. The helpless feeling of situations being out of control.

9

$\mathcal{G}$wen took inventory of the state of her clothing. Her dress and petticoats would take time to dry. She fluffed her skirt and lifted the hem slightly to allow warm air to reach her legs. There was no denying that falling into the icy water had been a shock.

She might have enjoyed Matt's attention except there was a little girl needing care.

He called, "Lindy." When there was no response, he called again. "Where can she be?"

The sharpness of his tone caused Gwen to wonder if he was annoyed or worried. She knew the answer. Both. And a touch of anger.

"She'll be cold and frightened." Would her words calm his anger?

"She should know better than to do that. She could have been hurt." His gaze returned to her. If only she could read his expression. "You could have been injured. As it is—"

"I'm not. Matt, remember she's just a little girl who is probably frightened at this moment. Poor child is likely aching for the comfort of her mother's arms."

His lips puffed out in a sigh. He rubbed the back of his neck. "You stay here. I'll find her." And with that, he trotted off.

Gwen thought of following but she wasn't ready to leave the comfort of the fire and wrapped the quilt more closely around her shoulders.

A snapping sound behind her sent a jolt of alarm up her veins. Who or what could it be and where was Matt when she needed him?

Slowly she turned. A dog stared at her from the shadows. The animal curled his lips in a snarl. This was no domestic creature. His low grumble sent shivers up her spine. The cold of river water expanded into icy fear.

She had not crossed the country, agreed to a month-long trial in anticipation of marriage to let it be taken from her by some wild thing. Not while she had breath to fight. Scrambling to her feet, she opened her arms, lifting the quilt in each hand and waved. "Shoo. Get away. Get." Her voice was loud and firm, though her insides quaked something fierce. She hollered again, louder.

The animal slunk away, glancing back twice as she continued to wave and shout.

"What's going on?"

Lowering her arms, she turned toward Matt. He held Lindy. "Am I ever glad to see you both." She rushed to his side relieved at his return and doubly relieved at seeing Lindy safe and sound.

Lindy held out her arms and Gwen took her. Although the child's dress was only damp in spots, she hurried to sit by the fire with Lindy in her arms. Matt followed and tightened the quilt around them both.

"I's sorry." Lindy's voice trembled.

"Honey, we're both all right and that's what matters."

"Uncle Matt said you could have been hurt."

"I'm not." Gwen lifted her gaze to Matt, hoping he would understand that she thought the child needed reassurance and comfort, not scolding.

His smile did not remove the tautness from his eyes. "Lindy and I had a talk and she agreed not to try flying again."

"But I can pretend from the ground."

Gwen chuckled. "Of course, you can."

Matt crouched beside them. "What were you yelling about a moment ago?"

"A wild dog. He was standing right there." She pointed. "And snarled at me."

"I'll check." Matt was gone before Gwen could beg him not to leave. She tightened her arms around Lindy and let the fire do its best to warm the blood flowing through her veins.

The snap and crackle of Matt's passage faded. She held her breath, listening. How far was the man going? She heard sounds again and a few minutes later, Matt returned.

"I didn't see anything, but I suspect it was a coyote. They are very curious but also easy to frighten away." He put more wood on the fire and then sat cross-legged beside them. "I'm not leaving until you two are dry."

Gwen's face and arms were warm. Her body and legs were cold. At the way he watched her, tenderness and concern in his expression, heat intensified in her heart. She didn't mind staying a while longer, enjoying Matt's company. He seemed more relaxed and welcoming today.

Matt looked around. "I used to come here with Corine."

Just like that, any sense of something special between them vanished. His thoughts were not on her but on his past love. She wouldn't allow herself to be disappointed. Not at all. She ducked her head to Lindy's hair. This child was why she was here. She hadn't forgotten that.

"Fact is," he continued. "We had a picnic here the last time I saw her. She left on the train that evening."

"I'm sorry." Though she was as sorry for herself as him. She'd been mistaken in thinking he was going out of his way to be kind to her.

He leaned forward, staring into the fire. "Corine was…" His voice trailed off.

She waited. Did she want to hear about the girl? What good would it do to be compared?

His burst of laughter startled her.

"Corine would have run home in tears if she'd fallen in the river. Maybe even taken to her bed for days." His gaze caught Gwen's and stalled there.

She couldn't break free. Not that she tried. Her cheeks warmed and it had nothing to do with the fire burning nearby. These flames came from inside and she allowed herself to believe he looked at her with surprised approval.

Or was it only surprise?

Lindy threw back the quilt and shifted to look into the trees where Gwen had seen the coyote. "Can I go look for him?"

"No, you cannot." Matt's words brooked no argument.

Gwen's arms tightened around the girl. "Stay and get dry."

Lindy let out a long-suffering sigh. "Can't have any fun around here."

At the child's morose tone, a smile crept across Gwen's face. Her gaze went to Matt. Her heart leaped at the amusement in his eyes. And something more. Or was that simply her wish? Maybe she'd fallen harder than she realized. That would explain how tangled her thoughts were.

Matt shifted and leaned back on one elbow to study her. It was all Gwen could do not to squirm at the way his gaze lingered.

"Should we be getting home?" she asked, unsure of what she should do or expect.

He sat up, his attention on the fire. "Are you in a hurry to return?"

Did she detect a hurt note in his tone? Did he really mean he wanted to stay here with her? And Lindy, of course.

"I have no reason to rush back but if you have things to do, I don't want to keep you from your work."

He grinned at her. "No one is forcing me to stay. I'll let you get dry. We should relax and enjoy ourselves."

That sounded about perfect to her.

"Can I have some more cookies?" Lindy asked.

Gwen didn't wait for an answer from Matt. "That's a good idea. Bring the tin here and we'll all have some." Providing food was a good reason to delay and enjoy.

Lindy brought the container. With Gwen's permission, she took two and went toward the water, seemingly content to study the ground at her feet. Was she looking for something? Gwen shrugged. About the only thing she'd find was rocks. She and Matt slowly ate cookies. She didn't want to hear any more about Corine and yet her mind raced with questions.

"You were telling me what Corine was like." So much for not wanting to hear more.

He was quiet for so long that she decided he wasn't going to answer her question and tried to tell herself she understood. She was about to say something to redirect the conversation when he started to speak, slowly and softly.

"Seems she was very young. Everything was new to her. Not something she always enjoyed. I remember one time the wagon got stuck in the mud and she began to cry. I asked why she was upset, and she said because she didn't want to have to get down and walk in the muck."

Another moment of silence. "Did she?" Gwen asked when it seemed he'd forgotten she was there.

He laughed. "I carried her to dry ground."

Gwen chuckled too although the sound did not come from her heart as she imagined a sweet young thing clutched in his arms.

"I look back and think we were both so young."

Gwen perked up. Was he voicing regrets?

"She was a city girl. I wonder how well she would have adapted to ranch life." He shook his head as if realizing it wouldn't have been all roses and honey. He directed his gaze to her. "I worried you might also find adjusting to be difficult."

"That's why you asked for a month for us to consider our decision." Her words barely rose above the music of the water flowing by, the melody echoing in her heart. He'd been thinking of her wellbeing.

He nodded. "I didn't want to make a mistake."

"Are you still concerned?" The question trembled from her lips. What if he said he was?

The corners of his mouth twitched. His eyes warmed. "I believe you enjoy country living." Before she could nod agreement, he shifted his attention to Lindy. "Your love for her is evident."

Her heart which had been blossoming at his confession that she fit into his life shrank like a sun-scorched flower. It was still only about Lindy.

Silence filled her mind. Disappointment stilled her thoughts.

"You must have had beaus. Anyone special."

"Why thank you." She grinned widely, pleasure straight from her heart filling her chest.

"For what?"

"For thinking I've had beaus."

"Didn't you?" He seemed puzzled by her response.

"A few."

"How many is a few?"

What harm did it do if she allowed herself to think he was the tiniest bit jealous? It helped her let go of the pain she felt at being so easily dismissed by her brother and by suitors that left so easily. As if she was of no importance.

She closed her eyes and pushed those thoughts behind walls. What point was there in regrets?

* * *

Of course, she'd had beaus. Probably dozens of them. Matt realized he'd clamped down on his teeth and forced his jaw to relax. The idea of her having the interest of young men didn't surprise him as much as knowing that not one of them had persuaded her to stay.

Which was to his advantage. She'd come west to marry him.

He sat up straighter and puffed out his chest.

"I had beaus. Nothing very serious, I suppose. At least, that's how it seemed." She stirred the flames with a twig and seemed taken by the task. Then she sighed and stopped. "When I was younger, I found boys immature. Their idea of fun was often mean-spirited. Then as I grew older, they were too serious. Sometimes it seemed they'd forgotten how to laugh." She gave him a crooked grin. "I guess I didn't know what I wanted." She returned to stirring the flames.

He didn't dare breathe as he thought of how confused she must have been. And yet now she appeared to know exactly what she wanted. A home that couldn't be snatched from her, she'd said. Marriage would provide that. If they both were still agreeable after a month, he could give her what she wanted. It was nice to think that he alone of her many suitors could provide for her needs.

She continued. "I guess I got used to what I had

and was too comfortable. I thought Maurice needed me. Would always need me. I knew my parents would want me to take care of him and I was glad to do so." She tossed the twig into the flames. "What a shock to realize he didn't and—as Patricia said—he just didn't know how to get free of me."

"Are you sure he felt that way or was that Patricia's opinion?"

Her gaze turned to meet his. Eyes wide and then narrowing as she considered his words. "He said he wanted me to stay so I suppose Patricia was only speaking her thoughts."

"You know, I can't help but think you're well to be away from her." He'd thought that before. She sounded like a nasty woman. Such a contrast to Gwen and her happy spirit. "She might have sucked the joy right out of you. And wouldn't that be a shame?"

Gwen's smile lit her eyes. "And wouldn't it have been?"

Their gazes held for several seconds. The air between them shimmered. He tried to dispel her hold over him. It was only the heat waves from the fire. And yet, the heady feeling left him slightly dizzy.

She shifted her skirts, spreading them to dry. "There was a time in the innocence of youth I loved a boy named Kenny Miner. I was seventeen. I turned to him when my mother and father died, hoping for support. I was devastated when he stopped calling. I guess he didn't see any future with a girl who had lost her parents and her home." Her brown eyes returned to his, darkness pooling in her irises. "I thought I could count on him to see my sorrow and my need and be there for me."

Matt felt her pain like an arrow piercing his chest. He didn't remember moving but suddenly he was next to her, his arm across her back, her head leaning on his shoulder. "Callow young man," he murmured and was rewarded with her soft laugh.

"I realize that now. But at the time..." She shrugged. "It was one more loss in my life and I felt like my heart had been ripped out."

He knew the feeling but to think she'd been hurt like that made him wish he'd been there. He would have stood by her.

"And then there was Wilson Lange. He was a friend of Maurice's and visited at our house. We courted for a few years. The friendship was comfortable. He came along with others but also on his own. We talked, played table games, and read to each other." Her gaze shifted from his slightly and she sighed softly.

"One day he announced he was heading to Canada and new opportunities. He halfheartedly asked if I wanted to accompany him, but I said I must stay and take care of Maurice. He left shortly after that without so much as a tender goodbye. I missed him something terrible." She sat back and stared at him. "I've often wondered if there's something wrong with me that no one..." She looked away. "Seems to value me." Her voice fell to a whisper.

He ran his gaze over her face, pausing at her full pink lips then returning to her eyes. "Upon close examination, I have to say I see nothing wrong with you." Had those husky words come from his mouth?

Her cheeks blossomed like June roses and a smile creased the corners of her eyes. She shifted out of his arms. He resisted the urge to pull her back, telling himself it was only to keep her warm.

She focused directly on him. "Just think. If Wilson had been more interested in me, I might now be living in Canada." Her gaze lingered for two heartbeats then shifted to Lindy who had collected a pile of rocks and sat rearranging them. "And then I wouldn't have the joy of taking care of her."

Lindy. It was the only reason he'd undertaken this mail-order bride business. And that's all it was... business.

Except at the moment, it didn't feel business-like.

Lindy jumped up and brought a handful of pebbles to Gwen. "See how pretty they are?" She held one up to the sunlight. "This one sparkles." She stared heaven-ward. "Just like angels in heaven." She ran back to her pile of rocks.

Matt reached to the side for another piece of wood he tossed on the fire. Gwen brought her attention back to him, surprise in her eyes.

"No rush to get home." He sat down beside her. "I

want to make sure you're good and dry before we return."

She smiled, sunshine and moonbeams in her eyes. "It's nice to sit here and enjoy the fire." Her voice fell to a whisper. "And the company."

When she didn't look Lindy's direction, he let himself believe she meant she enjoyed his presence. And why not? There was nothing wrong with his company.

"Did you go on picnics back in Kellom?" It was a silly question. Of course, she did. But he wanted to hear about her life before she'd come to marry him. Who did she go with? What did they do?

She rearranged her skirt again, shifting the fabric toward the fire. "I belonged to a group of young ladies who gathered with Mrs. Strong for Bible study. We went on a picnic two or three times a year. It was fun. Usually, we went a distance from the river. Our favorite spot was under a spreading tree that allowed us a wide viewpoint." She tipped her head and looked thoughtful. "It was nothing compared to looking out at Shannon Valley from the ranch."

The way she looked at him caused his heart to gently tip over like a puppy wanting to be patted.

"What about you, you must have gone on picnics?" Her gaze shifted away, leaving him disappointed. He dismissed the silly notion and concentrated on her words as she continued to speak.

"Wide open spaces to explore. I think you could go miles in any direction and find something new."

He chuckled. "What you call a picnic, we call work." He suddenly found things he wanted to tell her. "Pa would take the four of us out with him to check on the herd or sometimes simply to ride the range and explore. I haven't thought of that for years. At the time I thought he was making sure we knew every inch of the land but…." He paused as his thoughts took shape. "Maybe he was spending time with us for another reason."

She waited, her eyes full of patience and…

He didn't say anything more. It was downright silly to think she was interested in more than his stories… that she was interested in him.

He continued, "Every trip was a learning experience. He taught us how to survive in the mountains. He had a native friend who sometimes joined us and taught us so much." He leaned back, a sense of contentment flowing over him. "I have some good memories of those times."

"It sounds wonderful." Her eyes glistened with pleasure.

"One of these days I'll take you out and show you the land. You and Lindy." Though the child had been added as an afterthought.

"I'd like that." She sighed and rearranged her skirts again.

"Are you getting dry?"

"I am. Your talk of memories reminds me of the happy times we had when my parents were alive." Her gaze went past him into the distance. "I remember one particular time. The weather was abysmal. Father had decided it was wise to remain indoors. The house was cold with the bitter wind battering it, so we gathered in the parlor, sitting close to the fireplace. Father was in a pleasant mood and said it was nice to be together safe and sound. Mama made tea and we ate a few cookies as we enjoyed our tea. Our parents told us stories about their youth. Things we'd never heard before. We laughed often. It's hard to believe that they were both gone the following winter, but I cherish that day. I guess I've never since felt so—" She turned her hands palms up. "It sounds silly. Needy even. But that was the last time I felt so important to anyone."

Matt wanted to pull her into his arms and reassure her. It surprised him how much he longed to say he valued her. "You're important to Lindy."

The smile that curved Gwen's mouth failed to reach her eyes. "I'm grateful I can be here." Her gaze lingered a moment then she checked her skirts. "They're dry."

He glanced at the sky. How had the sun gotten so far to the west? "We should be on our way." He called Lindy, doused the fire thoroughly, and gathered up the picnic.

Lindy insisted on sitting between the two of them as they began the journey toward home. "I'm tired."

She yawned and stretched then turned to Gwen. "Can I sit on your knee?"

"Of course." Gwen settled the child with Lindy's head on her shoulder. In minutes, Lindy was asleep, sagging against Gwen's arm.

Knowing how heavy the four-year-old could become, Matt shifted closer. "Let some of her weight rest on me."

Gwen whispered, "Thank you," as she leaned against him.

Matt bent to kiss the top of Lindy's head. He lingered a heartbeat, wishing this could... He sat up. He didn't wish for anything except for someone to love and care for Lindy. So why did it feel like he'd been robbed of something?

10

It was late by the time they reached the ranch. Gwen shook Lindy as they stopped in front of the house. A whiny protest indicated her resistance to being disturbed. Matt took her from Gwen, and put her on the ground before he reached up to Gwen.

Gwen missed the warmth of the little girl in her arms. Even as she regretted that Matt no longer sat pressed to her side. She'd enjoyed the day in his company. He'd seemed more relaxed.

Was he seeing her as the bride he'd chosen? The mother for Lindy that he wanted? A woman who would warm his home and care for his needs? Three more weeks until he gave his decision. Unless he changed his mind before then.

She carried Lindy inside as Matt drove the wagon away. She'd informed him she'd have something ready for a late supper as soon as he returned. Thanks to a well-stocked pantry, she hoped she could accomplish that. Canned navy beans, a variety of vegetables, and a few well-chosen spices soon simmered together in a savory-scented soup. She quickly mixed biscuits and put them in the oven.

"Lindy, could you please—?" But Lindy was gone. Gwen caught a glimpse of her racing down the path. Likely going to check on the kittens.

A short time later, golden biscuits cooled on the cupboard. The soup was ready, and a taste had proven it was as good as it smelled. The table was set. At the sound of Lindy's voice, she glanced out the window. Matt and Lindy walked side by side toward the house, Lindy chattering and laughing.

Gwen watched them approach, the sight warming her heart. The child might be an orphan, but she was well-loved. Not only by the men of the ranch. Gwen's heart swelled with affection for the little girl.

Her gaze shifted to Matt. He grinned at something Lindy said. Gwen's breath caught in her lungs, trapped by the surging response of her heart as she eyed the man she planned to wed. She jerked from the window and pressed her hands to her stomach as if she could contain the turmoil within. She pressed harder and forced her lungs to work.

They'd agreed to a marriage in name only. It was what she wanted as much as he. It would give her a home where she could count on permanency. She hadn't changed her mind. Nor did she mean to.

The back door opened and closed, and the pair entered the kitchen. "Smells mighty fine in here," Matt said.

She allowed herself only a glance and the quickest of smiles before she turned to the stove. "Supper is ready." She filled a soup tureen and carried it to the table and placed a platter of warm biscuits beside it. Her emotions were back where they belonged. Her unsettledness was only because he'd been so kind this afternoon and she'd enjoyed the outing so much. Reminding herself that he'd promised to take them on a picnic out on the range gave her hope they might repeat the experience.

He said grace and tasted the food. "You cook as good as my mother did."

"I take that as the highest praise." She met his gaze and let herself dwell there one, two, three seconds. Or more.

"You should." He waved his spoon in the air. "That is not to say Merry wasn't a good cook. And even Wally can cook up steaks like no one else. But your food is different."

"Different? How?" She wasn't sure that was a compliment despite his earlier praise.

"You make so many good things."

Lindy bounced forward to the edge of her chair. "Can you make rice pudding? Like Mama made."

"I can make rice pudding, but I'll tell you a secret." She leaned over to whisper to Lindy. "No one will ever make it like your mama's. Do you know why?"

Her eyes big, Lindy shook her head.

"Because it was made with your mama's love and no one else can do that."

Lindy blinked several times and swallowed hard. Gwen wondered if she should have reminded the child of her mother. Not that she thought Lindy would ever forget. She knew what it was like. The memory hovering close. Sometimes a gossamer mist, full of sweetness and light. Other times a dark cloud that shut out the sun and chilled the bones.

Gwen glanced at Matt to see if she'd said the wrong thing and incurred his displeasure. But he watched Lindy, waiting for her response.

Lindy sucked in a noisy breath. "I guess that's right. Papa said no one could cook like Mama." She finished the last bite of her biscuit before she added hope-filled words. "But I might like your rice pudding too."

Gwen laughed. "Then I shall make some and let you decide."

Matt chuckled. "Something to look forward to."

"What is a favorite thing your mother made?" she asked him. "Maybe I can make my version of it."

"Well, I don't know." His gaze drifted to her, but she guessed he wasn't seeing her but something in his past. She didn't blink. Didn't move, not wanting to break this tenuous connection between them. "I know. Lardie cake. You ever made it?"

"I have. It was one of my father's favorite delicacies." She liked the idea of a shared special treat. "It seems I'll be busy tomorrow. Oh, wait." She sat back. "Tomorrow is Sunday."

"We'll go to church. We usually have the noon meal shortly after we return."

Her thoughts raced. Normally, she would have done some preparation on Saturday, but the day was already gone. What could she make that would be ready for Sunday dinner?

Matt pressed his palm to his forehead. "I plumb forgot. Wally said he'd planned a meal for us all tomorrow. So you don't have to do anything."

"I'll be better prepared next time."

"I'm done. Can I go?" Lindy looked like an anxious bird about to take flight.

Gwen glanced at Matt. He was shaking his head. She agreed.

"Honey," she said. "It's late. Time for you to get ready for bed."

"Ahh, do I have to?"

Gwen hugged the child. "Would you like us to read your book to you again? Or should I find the Bible story book I brought?"

"Can I do both?"

"Yes, if you hurry."

Lindy reached her room before Gwen finished

speaking. Gwen couldn't help but see the humor in Lindy's hurry. Gracious, the girl loved her stories. As she glanced around the room, Matt's unbroken attention caught her completely. Before warmth could spread from her neck to her cheeks, he looked away and the moment fractured into a million pieces.

"Goodness." She hurried to her feet. "I'd better get the table cleaned before she's back."

"I'll help." They worked in unison, taking dirty dishes to the basin of hot water. Their hands touched as she handed him a wet plate to dry. It was all she could do not to jerk away. What was wrong with her that suddenly his presence put her off balance and the slightest touch jarred her like being struck by lightning?

Lindy returned, shifting impatiently from one foot to the other before the last spoon was back in the drawer. She held her new book to her chest.

Gwen hurried to get the other book from her trunk, taking a moment to breathe deeply and regain her composure. Why was she acting so foolishly? She'd known she'd share a home with Matt when she left Kellom. She'd understood there'd be awkwardness from time to time as they moved around each other. She reasoned they'd get used to it. What she hadn't realized was that there would be moments of acute awareness.

She'd get used to that too. After a bit.

A few minutes later, they had read to Lindy and

Gwen heard her prayers with half her attention, listening to Matt move about in the living room. The thought of rejoining him sent shimmers of excitement through her. Or was it nervousness?

But when she returned, Matt stood at the door. "I'll say good night."

The shimmering stopped. Her skin grew taut. Seems he couldn't wait to rush away. "Thank you for the pleasant afternoon. I really enjoyed it." She barely got the words from her mouth before he ducked out the door. She stared at the wooden barrier. "Well, at least we won't be awkwardly bumping into each other or worrying about what to say."

Determined to force her thoughts to normal things, she finished cleaning the kitchen and then sat in the rocking chair, her Bible in her lap. But she kept losing her place on the page as her mind wandered. The awkward and abrupt ending left her thoughts twisting. Had she put more importance on their time together than it warranted?

Remember you are only here to be a mother to Lindy. You agreed the marriage would be in name only.

SUNDAY MORNING DAWNED golden and bright. Because they hadn't bathed Saturday, Gwen rose early to heat water so they could both have a sponge bath. She dried Lindy's hair as best she could by the stove, brushed it out, and braided it from the top of Lindy's head.

Her own hair hung loose in the hopes it would dry before they had to leave for church.

Breakfast was ready to serve when Matt stepped into the house. He ground to a halt and stared. Heat raced up Gwen's neck and not from the stove. She touched her hair. "I need to let it dry." It was all she could do not to scoop it up and secure it at the back of her head.

He swallowed audibly and nodded.

Forcing her attention to the task at hand, she carried the food to the table.

Lindy barely waited for Matt's amen before she tossed her head sending her braid flying across her face.

"Uncle Matt, do you like my hair?"

Matt narrowed his eyes and studied the child. "Have you done something with it?"

Lindy sat back with a huff. "It's braided like Mama used to do."

Matt blinked. "Why so it is." He grinned and Gwen realized he was teasing. "How'd you manage that?"

Lindy huffed again. "Auntie Gwen did it." She turned her head and flung the braid once more. "It's nice, isn't it?"

Matt patted Lindy's head. "It's very nice."

Lindy beamed. "I know."

Matt's gaze came to Gwen, swept over her face,

taking in her hair. Her pulse beat in her neck, suffusing her cheeks which she felt blaze with heat.

He cleared his throat and turned back to his breakfast allowing Gwen to ease air into her lungs. Finished, he pushed from the table. "I'll be back in half an hour to pick you up."

She stared after him. Was she imagining he'd left in a hurry? Only one explanation came to mind. Seeing her with her hair loose had unsettled him. Her eyes crinkled with secret amusement. It was time he saw her as more than a mother for Lindy.

When the wagon rattled to the door, she and Lindy went out to join the others. Matt's brothers and Wally sat in the back and Lindy jumped in to join them. Matt held out a hand to assist her to the seat. "Your hair is up."

Did he sound surprised? Pleased? She wished she knew. "I wouldn't go to church with it down."

"Humph. I kind of liked it that way." His words were barely more than a whisper as if he didn't want the others to overhear.

She positioned herself on the wooden bench and stared at the rumps of the horses. He liked her hair down...an acknowledgment of her hope he had begun to see her for herself.

They arrived at the church and trooped in—she found amusement in the tromp of five pairs of boots on the wooden floor. Matt stepped aside and waited for his brothers and Wally to slide into one pew then indicated she should go to the one behind. Holding Lindy's hand, she took her place with Matt sitting on the other side of Lindy. Several people looked her way, but no one stared.

The preacher rose. Pastor Ingram—the man who was supposed to have married Gwen and Matt. His gaze rested on her with softness and welcome. It was like a benediction.

The songs were familiar and the reading of God's word as warm and comforting as a familiar blanket. Pastor Ingram spoke from the twenty-third Psalm. Reminding them of God's great care.

Gwen drew the words into her soul. God had brought her here to a place of green pastures and still waters. As Pastor Ingram prayed his closing prayer, she added her own words. *Thank you for bringing me here. I love the landscape. I love the ranch and Lindy. I even—*

She stopped at that. No point in being greedy.

As they filed out, people greeted her, and Matt introduced the neighbors. Mostly married couples or cowboys—from young to old. Everyone welcomed her. A couple of the cowboys might have held her hand longer than acceptable but moved on when Matt cleared his throat.

The last of the congregants departed and Mrs. Ingram joined Gwen and the circle of Shannon cowboys.

"Matt, I've been thinking about this situation. Mrs.

Strong trusted me to see that Miss Humber was properly taken care of. She'd be shocked to learn I've failed. I spoke to Mr. Ingram about it. He's agreed to perform the ceremony today."

No one moved or said anything as her words fell like crashing rocks.

"But Ma'am—" Matt began when he'd recovered from her announcement.

Mrs. Ingram forged on not giving him a chance to finish. "Have you found her acceptable?" The woman faced the circle of men. "Your brothers are here. Do any of you have a reason Miss Humber isn't suitable as Matt's wife?"

"No, ma'am," they mumbled, shifting from foot to foot.

"Then I see no need for delay." It seemed the matter was settled in her mind.

"We agreed to a month." The way Matt's eyes darkened, Gwen knew he wasn't about to change his mind. No matter what the preacher's wife said. "I have to make sure she's right for Lindy."

For Lindy? Nothing more? Gwen's world crashed into bits and pieces. While she'd been dreaming that he might value her as a person, he clung to his need— his only need— a mother for the little girl.

Mrs. Ingram jabbed her finger at Matt. "And in another three weeks what are you thinking will happen? That she'll suddenly turn into a shrew? Or disappear with your coffee can of savings?" She confronted the others again. "Do any of you have a reason that this wedding should be delayed?"

They all mumbled *no* as they shuffled their feet and kept their heads down before this woman. Matt squirmed as if his skin had grown too tight.

Gwen covered her mouth but couldn't contain the amusement rushing up her throat. She laughed so hard her eyes watered.

Luke grinned. Riley wouldn't look at her. Andy seemed confused as if wondering if he'd missed something. Poor Wally chewed his bottom lip, but she could see in his eyes that he understood the humor of the situation.

Gwen brought her gaze to Matt. His eyes were hard. Did he feel the preacher's wife had ambushed him? Understanding how he might fear disaster, wonder if he could trust the future, wonder more than anything if he could trust her, laughter ended on a gulp, and she sobered.

She knew what she must do to show he could count on her. "Mrs. Ingram, I appreciate your concern, but I agreed to a month, and I mean to keep my word." Her eyes steady, she directed her gaze to Matt. Would he appreciate her decision?

Before she could assess his reaction, Mrs. Ingram grabbed her hand and dragged her away from the others.

Lindy raced around the perimeter of the yard,

arms out like a bird, thankfully unaware of the drama taking place a few yards away.

"My dear, you don't have to agree to living there like this...with all those men." She shook her hand in their direction like trying to rid herself of a bug.

Gwen caught her arm to stop her. "Mrs. Ingram, you know all of them—the Shannon brothers and Wally. Do you really think they would take advantage of me?"

She swallowed hard. "No, but—"

"There you go. Let us work out things our way."

"What am I supposed to say to Mrs. Strong?"

"Tell her I arrived safely and am enjoying life on the ranch. I'm going to write her too and assure her all is well." She should have written already and to Maurice as well. "Now if you'll excuse me, the men are anxious to get home." She patted the woman's hand, called Lindy, and made her way to the wagon. The men scrambled to get into the back and Matt helped Gwen to the seat.

As they drove from town, the humor of the situation again filled Gwen and she laughed.

"I felt like a cornered rat," Matt grumbled but he barely got the words out before the others chortled.

MATT GATHERED with his brothers around the table at the big house, still smarting a little at Mrs. Ingram's insistence that he and Gwen marry immediately. He understood her concerns, but he had matters of his own that must be addressed. Namely, would Gwen stay? Would she prove a good mother to Lindy? That was what mattered.

Luke leaned over the table. "Poor Mattie," he said with a great deal of amusement in his voice. "He was ready to go hide under a rock."

Riley grunted. "Can't say as I blame him. A man don't like being bullied into something."

"Thanks, Riley." Matt appreciated knowing his older brother understood how uncomfortable the situation had made him.

Andy stirred the stew on his plate without bringing any of it to his mouth. "Why'd you ask her to come out here if you didn't intend to marry her?"

Luke didn't give Matt a chance to answer. "My offer still stands, Gwen. If Matt isn't going to marry you, I'll take his place."

Matt planted his fists on either side of his plate. "If anyone marries her, it will be me. We've agreed to a delay simply to test the waters and make sure it's right for us." It gave her room for second thoughts but far better to know for sure. A tiny thought ticked at the back of his head. Could he ever be certain? Certain that people would stay? That bad things wouldn't happen? That he could protect those in his care?

He sucked in a hot breath. He meant to do his best

to insure exactly that. "Why is everyone so upset about it?"

"Food's getting cold." Wally's words brought them back to the meal he'd prepared.

When dinner had been consumed, Lindy and Gwen helped clean up. Luke caught Matt's elbow and dragged him outside. "What is wrong with you? You heard what Mrs. Ingram said and I guarantee she isn't the only one to hold that opinion. Why don't you marry her instead of making her wait? It's not like she isn't perfectly suitable for you. In fact—" He looked past Matt to the house where Gwen washed dishes. "She might be too good for you."

Matt crossed his arms over his chest. He didn't have to answer to Luke or anyone. "She agreed."

"Did she have a choice?"

"Of course, she did."

Luke leaned back and considered Matt. Matt held his gaze. They'd done this staring thing many times. He could outlast Luke any day.

"Tell me." Luke's words were soft. "What would you have done if she refused to delay the wedding a month? Would you have sent her back? Left her in town?"

Matt didn't have to give Luke an answer. He knew in his mind why he'd asked to wait but he didn't expect anyone to understand that he needed to be sure that...What? That he could guarantee the future? Make it safe?

He shook his head. Where were those arguments coming from? He didn't need them...wasn't prepared to listen to them. His decision had been made with Lindy's best interests in mind.

"Lindy needs her." Luke took one step away. "You need her." He strode toward the barn.

Matt began to follow then changed his mind. What did he need her for except to make a home for Lindy?

It wasn't as if *he* needed a home. Or anything else. No sir. He preferred to keep thoughts of love out of his head.

Love? Who'd said anything about that? Love meant pain. He wasn't going that route again. Ever.

11

---

*G*wen left the house and stopped when she
saw Matt. He stood a few feet away, his
arms crossed as he stared at Luke heading
toward the barn. She could feel the tension in the air.
Was it because of her? She didn't want to be the cause
of strife between the brothers. What was that verse in
the Bible? In Proverbs somewhere. One of the six
things the Lord hated. *He that soweth discord among
brethren.*

Matt joined her and they returned to their house.
Their house? His continued insistence in delaying their
marriage sent doubt skittering through her brain. Was
she unknowingly failing in some direction?

He cleared his throat. "I apologize for the scene at
church."

She digested his words. "Can I hope that I'll pass
your test?"

He stopped. Blinked. "It wasn't a test. It was as much for your sake as mine. I wouldn't want you to be unhappy stuck out here."

The idea of her not wanting to be there was so ludicrous she laughed. She didn't need time to think about this decision, but uncertainty fluttered through her. Would the delay give him an opportunity to decide she didn't meet his standards? A distant ache, one she tried to ignore, reminded her of the times she had not been enough for others. She shook her head as if she could throw off those thoughts. "I can't think of any place I'd sooner be. The view is stunning. I love Lindy. And there's lots of pleasant company."

"Good to know," Matt said, meeting her gaze.

The air between them grew shiny. In the distance, a crow cawed. Closer to them, Lindy sang and whirled in the dust.

He broke free of the look first. "I promised to show you the valley. Would you like to do that this afternoon?"

Grateful that the discussion and the uncertainty were to be set aside, she answered, "I'd love to. Give me a moment to change out of my Sunday clothes." She called Lindy and they hurried to the house.

Matt waited in the kitchen a few minutes later when Gwen left her bedroom. He stared out the window. She drew to a halt at the expression on his face. Did she see regret? He turned at her approach and his face lit. "I was thinking of all the things to show you down there."

Nice to know he was eager to spend the afternoon with her, showing her his world. "I'm looking forward to seeing it all."

Lindy raced from her bedroom, her braid flapping against her back. She was out the door, the adults following at a more leisurely pace. They passed Luke's house and continued along the path. The valley floor lay beneath them, the water at the bottom shimmering with reflected sunshine.

Gwen swung her arms at her side and smiled as the light echoed in her heart. She loved it here and would prove she belonged.

The trail turned toward the bank and slanted downward.

"Lindy, you stay behind us," Matt called.

The child stopped and obediently waited for the adults to go ahead. Matt went first, taking sideways steps as he reached out a hand to Gwen. For a heartbeat, she hesitated, remembering how her heart and mind had reacted previously. Even at innocent touches. But the trail was steep. She needed his help. And what better excuse to hold his hand and assess her reaction. Was it anything more than strangeness?

She clung to him as they eased down the path, but her uncertain footing gave her no time to dwell on her feelings.

"Take it slow," he counseled. "Never rush. And

never go down this trail after a rain. In fact,"–he stopped moving – "Promise me you'll never go down here without me or one of the men to take you." He waited, his gaze lifted to hers.

Dizziness filled her head, and she gripped his hand more tightly. It had to be because of their position on the side of the valley. Not because of the way his eyes implored her. "I promise."

He turned back to navigating the trail and her dizziness passed. It was only that it felt good to think he cared about her well-being. *Don't be silly. Of course, he does.* If she wasn't there, he'd have to find someone else to care for Lindy.

The idea of another woman loving and caring for either of them shafted through her like a blunt arrow and she groaned.

He stopped and turned. "What's wrong?"

Not willing to share the awful truth she'd just acknowledged, she shook her head. "It's a long way down."

"The path improves in a few steps."

She glanced back to check on Lindy who clung to the bushes beside the trail without any sign of fear and stared up. "A big bird." Her voice was full of awe.

Gwen followed the direction of her gaze and saw a huge bird with a distinctive white head lift from a nearby branch.

"A bald eagle," Matt informed them, and they watched as the bird soared higher and higher.

It was almost out of sight before Gwen drew in an overdue breath. "That was wonderful. It reminds me of a Bible verse." She gulped at the one that had sprung to her mind. *The way of an eagle in the air; the way of a serpent upon a rock; the way of a ship in the midst of the sea; and the way of a man with a maid.* She was not about to mention that one. Instead, she quoted, "'But they that wait upon the LORD shall renew their strength; they shall mount up with wings as eagles; they shall run, and not be weary; and they shall walk, and not faint.'"

"Does that mean God will make us fly?"

She chuckled at Lindy's question though a thread of alarm accompanied it. "Only birds fly."

Lindy shook her head. "Some day I'll fly."

Gwen didn't argue. No doubt the child was thinking of her parents and how they'd 'flown' to heaven. From what Lindy had said, Gwen understood that Mrs. Ingram had informed her that some day she would fly up to heaven too. In due time, Gwen silently added.

They reached the bottom and Matt went to help Lindy.

A strange feeling swept over Gwen. Like she hovered at the edge of a black hole. She looked skyward and her world righted. Lindy scampered fearlessly down the trail, refusing Matt's outstretched hand. Once on level ground she raced ahead, flapping her arms.

Her thoughts still teetering on the brink of some-thing unfamiliar, Gwen focused on Lindy. "Has she always had such a fascination with flying?"

"Not that I'm aware of. Do you think it means something?"

They stood side by side, observing the child who seemed carefree and happy. Finally, Gwen answered. "I don't know if it means anything, but I don't see any harm in it. She seems content enough."

"I couldn't ask for more."

She pressed her hand to his arm. It was as if she couldn't help herself. Always wanting to touch him even though it did such strange things to her equilib-rium. "She must miss them even more than you do."

He brought his gaze to her hand then slowly lifted his head to meet her eyes. A frisson of awareness engulfed her. Her mouth dried and, feeling awkward and off balance, she drew her hand away. As heat flooded her face, she ducked her head hoping he wouldn't notice the color that must surely be branding her cheeks.

"Come on, you need to see everything." He took a step away. It took three breaths before she was free of her confusion. Grateful for normalcy, she walked with him to the edge of the water.

"It's just a creek though Pa insisted it was a river. It's slow and murky by August but clear and cold this time of year." He bent and scooped up a handful to his mouth. "Try it."

She did, surprised at how cold it was and how refreshing. He grinned at her reaction.

Lindy rejoined them and took Gwen's hand. "Come on." With a child on one side and a big, strong man on the other, Gwen allowed herself to be drawn along. She didn't think anything they showed her could compete with the feeling of this moment.

Perhaps one thing would make it better. If Matt took her hand. Or would that confuse her so she couldn't enjoy the scenery? *Guess I'll never know.* She laughed at her foolishness and knowing Matt would wonder what amused her, she lifted her head heavenward. "It's all so beautiful and unbelievable. Almost like walking in the Garden of Eden."

His eyes flashed approval. "Maybe Pa should have named it Eden Valley." He pulled his mouth down into a gesture of concentration and shook his head. "Nah. Pa wouldn't give up the chance to have his name forever remembered by calling it Shannon Valley."

His answer tickled her clear through and she laughed. His deeper tones joined her and for a moment, she reveled in the joy of shared amusement.

Lindy tugged Gwen's hand and she turned her attention back to the scene. Ahead of them, the stream widened, the water slowed.

"It's a natural dam," Matt explained. "The water is deep enough to swim in."

"Isn't it cold?"

He waggled his eyebrows. "Feels perfect on a hot summer day."

Unable to look at him and keep her equilibrium she glanced upward. The windows of a house twinkled in the sun.

Matt followed the direction of her gaze. "Luke's house. Come, I'll show you where you can see our house."

She held the word *our* close as she accompanied him to the spot indicated and saw the windows winking at her. "It's beautiful." Beyond that, she saw the big house. "I don't see Riley's place."

"We'd have to cross the creek to see it. We'll do that another time."

In her heart, Gwen placed the promise of more time together in a special, secret corner. They continued, meandering along the valley floor. They paused to examine little red flowers and a nest of tiny eggs. Matt couldn't tell her what bird had laid them. A bunny hopped out of sight. They reached a spot where a natural earthen bench provided a place to sit.

Lindy perched there. "Mama and Papa brought me here once. We had a picnic. Mama let me eat four cookies." She held up her fingers to indicate.

Matt tickled her under the chin. "Four? Did you leave any for your papa?"

She nodded, her expression serious. "He ate six!"

Gwen chuckled at Lindy's shocked tone. Her gaze

met Matt's and she caught a flash of humor tinged with pain.

Lindy wandered away leaving Matt and Gwen sitting on the grass-covered bench.

"Roscoe was my best friend." Matt's voice was heavy with emotion. "We often went swimming together." His gaze went to the dammed-up water. "We would have races. Swimming races, foot races, and horse races." His gaze went to the distance seeing the past, not the present. "He used to be pretty wild. Guess marriage settled him down."

Gwen didn't respond, understanding that he was sorting through his memories.

He slowly released his breath. "I miss him a lot."

Ignoring the warning in her heart that said she wasn't doing this for his sake alone, she took his hand and squeezed it. He turned his palm toward hers and held on as if finding it comforting and she let herself believe she could give him what he needed in more ways than as a housekeeper.

Warmth flowed up her arm. She hoped it was also flowing up his and into his heart. To comfort him, of course. No other reason. Certainly not a wish that he would look at her and see a woman.

Stop right there, Gwendolyn Humber. You knew from the start what you agreed to. You had no objection. So don't build up paper walls of hope and expectation that will disintegrate before the winds of truth.

What was the truth? That she was easily replaced

or forgotten though she knew of nothing she'd done to make such actions so easy. She slipped her hand from his and knotted it to the other in her lap. A marriage in name only would guarantee permanency. The month's delay was not just a chance to prove herself, it assured her that he would make a commitment that stuck. After all, he'd see her good points and if she had her way, he wouldn't see any bad ones. At least nothing beyond minor things like a tendency to oppose him. Or forgetting a pie in the oven.

They stayed there a long time just talking. He told her of the excitement on the ranch when Lindy was born. The way people at church had clustered around the infant the first time they took her there. "You'd think they never saw a baby," Roscoe had said. Then laughed. "Of course, they never saw one as sweet as Lindy."

In turn, she told him about her friends back in Kellom. He wanted to know what they'd done for entertainment.

"We gathered at the parsonage to study the Bible. There were six of us who attended regularly for years. Others came and left. Mostly because the pretty girls got married and had babies."

He tipped his head to consider her at that comment. "You know pretty doesn't mean a good person, don't you?"

She lifted her hands in resignation. He'd as good as said she wasn't pretty. And even though she'd told him that in one of her letters, it wasn't something a woman liked to hear especially from a man she intended to marry.

"Besides, who said you aren't pretty?" he asked with a bit of a laugh.

Her mouth fell open and she stared at him.

He touched her head. "You were real pretty with your hair down." Were his words husky?

She closed her mouth and blinked. Had he really said that? What did it mean? "Thank you," she managed to stammer before she shifted her gaze away to stare at the light flashing on the rippling water.

"Sorry, didn't mean to make you uncomfortable."

"No, no." She forced herself to look at him. "It's just that no one's ever said anything like that to me."

"Not even your parents?"

"They didn't believe in praising us. I heard them say they didn't want us to get swelled heads."

"Someone must have praised you, surely."

A smile full of sweetness curved her mouth. "I told you that Mama said I was her special gift from heaven bringing her so much joy—her ray of sunshine." That had always made her feel cherished. A distant memory surfaced. "And one time we saw a street performer playing the flute. Such cheerful music. I stood before him and drank it in. Swaying and moving to the tune. He stopped and said, 'Little girl, never lose your joy.' I might have lost it temporarily a few times but never permanently."

He caught her hand and cradled it between his. "I hope you never do. I like hearing you laugh."

She couldn't think. Couldn't find a word to respond. If she needed a reason to believe marriage to this man was a good idea, this afternoon and yesterday had provided it. Even more so, his words. And now the way he held her hand as if she mattered to him. And not just as a mother for Lindy.

She was thinking of a real marriage. He'd only offered a pretend one. And she'd agreed. Wishing for anything more was foolish.

She bolted to her feet. "We need to keep up with Lindy."

HE'D EMBARRASSED her yet again. And it wasn't a bit like him. He never talked about feelings. He never paid compliments. It was something Corine had chastised him for. How often had she insisted he say something nice about her hair or her dress?

Thankfully, Lindy pulled Gwen along, the two of them laughing. Matt hung back, enjoying the moment. The sun was warm on their shoulders, the heavens so blue.

He caught up to them. "Look at the sky. Pa called it Montana blue."

She stopped to look upward. "Montana blue. I like

that." She fell into step beside him. "I think I'll call this afternoon Montana pleasure."

He chuckled. "Pa would have liked you." He was sure both his parents would have approved of her. Thinking of his parents triggered a thought that had been hovering in the back of his head.

"Remember I said that angel picture in Lindy's book was the same as one in Mother's Bible?"

"I remember."

"I located her Bible and have begun reading it." He didn't know when he'd neglected doing so nor why.

They stopped walking, and he led her to a grassy place to sit down before he continued.

"I recall that I often found her reading it. Seems the Good Book was never far from her. While she was alive, she read us a portion every evening."

"That sounds nice."

"The practice stopped after her passing. I suppose Pa discovered it hard to continue something that she'd always done." An unfamiliar truth rose in his heart. "I know Ma would be disappointed that I haven't continued reading the Bible as she taught."

He turned to face Gwen because what he was about to say was important to him and he wanted to make certain she understood. Even more, he hoped she'd approve of his suggestion.

"Once we're married, I'd like to follow her practice and have family Bible reading every day in our home."

"I'd like that." A gentle, sweet smile accompanied

her words. "I believe that putting God first is the surest way to a happy home."

"Then we are agreed?"

"We are. In fact, we don't have to wait until we're married. We could start tonight." She lowered her gaze. "If you'd like?" Her eyes came to him, brimming with hope and—

He had no idea what he thought he saw. Or did he mean, what he wished he'd see?

Lindy trotted up to them, planted her hands on her hips, and squinted. "You gonna stay there all day?"

He and Gwen looked at each other and laughed. Their shared amusement honeyed his insides.

"We're coming." He rose and held out a hand to Gwen. He only meant to help her to her feet, but she made no effort to pull away and he didn't release her as they walked along the valley floor. It felt right and good.

"How far does this go?" she asked.

"The valley widens out in five miles and then it's nothing but a gently rolling hill. We used to ride there and camp." They rounded a curve. "You can see what I mean in the distance."

She cupped her free hand to her eyes and stared. "I'm more accustomed to seeing a wide ribbon of water. It's so different to see green grass."

He let her take her time studying the landscape.

"I could never get tired of this." Her face shone with inner joy as she looked at him. She seemed about to say something then changed her mind. Instead, she shifted her gaze to the west. "Look, the sun is resting against the rim."

How had it gotten so late? "Lindy, come. We need to get back."

The little girl returned to them, carrying a handful of feathers she'd picked up. The return trip was rushed as he urged them to a fast pace. He waited until Lindy ran ahead to explain to Gwen. "We need to get up the trail before it's so shadowed we can't see."

She broke into a trot. "Are we in danger?"

"I didn't mean to frighten you. We'll have to be careful, that's all." He didn't point out that being familiar with the terrain, he could do it easily enough. They reached the upward path in less time than the outward journey had taken. He let Lindy go first, warning her not to rush and to hang on to the bushes.

"You go ahead," he instructed Gwen. He'd be able to catch her if she stumbled.

The first part of the trail was relatively easy and then they bent forward as it grew steeper. He kept one arm stretched out, a poor barrier to the yawning edge but he'd do his best to stop her from falling should she stumble.

Her foot slipped and he caught her around the waist. For seconds he pressed her to his chest as his heart hammered. As it settled, he thought how perfectly she fit into his arms. How sweet she smelled.

Her hair tickled his nose, and he had an urge to pull the pins out and let it hang free.

She righted herself. "Thanks. I'll be more careful."

He sucked in air like a man surfacing from being stuck in deep water. "Take your time. Grab the bushes like Lindy is doing." The child was almost lost in the shadows until her head crested the rim and the sunlight brightened her.

"Almost there." He hoped his words calmed Gwen.

She stepped to the top and stood beside Lindy. The lowering sun blazed on her face. He almost fell backward at the way her countenance glowed, more light coming from inside her than from the sun.

"The sunlight is touching everything with gold."

He completed the climb and stood at her side, looking at the sky although it was all he could do to keep his eyes off her.

"I'm hungry." Lindy was on the point of getting whiney.

"Let's go home." Gwen reached a hand to the child and the three of them returned to the house. "I don't have anything prepared." She sounded apologetic. "But I can make something quick."

"Take your time. I have a couple of things to do."

He went to his room in the big house and lifted Mother's Bible from the table by his bed.

Andy entered the house just as Matt reached the door. He looked at the Bible in Matt's hands. "Thought you were only borrowing it."

"Gwen would like it if we read it after supper."

Andy rocked back and forth on his heels. "Like Ma did?"

"Do you mind?"

Andy still stared at the Bible. "I think Ma would like that." He raised his gaze to Matt's. "I don't think you should wait to marry Gwen."

"Why's that?" He kept his tone mild. Not that he expected that he fooled Andy.

"Because I like her."

Matt snorted. "You've seen her what? Two times?"

"More'n that. We all rode to church together. Besides, I know what I see."

Matt wasn't going to ask what his younger brother thought. Yet the words came from his mouth. "And what exactly is it you think you see?"

"She smiles a lot. Lindy likes her. I can smell good food cooking over there. Now don't tell me you didn't notice."

"Of course, I noticed. I'm not an idiot."

Andy gave a sly grin. "Well, if you want to believe that..." He narrowed his eyes. "So why don't you marry her?"

Why indeed? She was proving to be a suitable person, but he couldn't escape the warning in the depths of his heart. Could he trust her to keep Lindy safe? Even louder came an unexpected question. Could he keep Gwen safe? His feet pounded down the path toward home, driving foolish questions from his head.

Matt sucked in cleansing air before he stepped into the peace of his own house. Pa was right to think they all needed their own place. Though Pa had in mind something other than the four of them living alone. At least he, of all the Shannon brothers, was doing as Pa wished. He ignored the protest in his brain that Pa meant more than bringing a woman into his home. There was Lindy too, he pointed out.

At his entrance, Gwen looked up with a welcoming smile. And immediately his troubles disappeared. He was at peace. It was a good thing no one could hear his thoughts and demand an explanation because he had none.

He sat down and ate although he couldn't say what it was that he put in his mouth. His attention was on vainly attempting to sort out the thoughts tangled in his head.

The meal over, he brought the Bible to the table. "This is Mother's Bible. Do you want to read it?"

"Would you?" she asked.

"I'd be honored. Where do you suggest I begin?"

"I've heard the beginning is a great place to start."

With a chuckle, he opened the book to Genesis and read the first chapter.

Slowly, reverently he closed the Bible and looked up to see both Lindy and Gwen with their eyes riveted to him. "I feel like I should close in prayer."

Gwen's gentle smile made him think of butterfly wings. "I'd like that."

"God, we thank You that You made the world and everything in it. Thank You for making it so beautiful." He wanted to add thanks for the people in his home and his brothers, too, of course. But sudden uncertainty made the words stick in his throat. "Amen."

"Didn't God make the birds?" Lindy asked.

Gwen seemed to understand what the child meant. "The Bible calls them fowl of the air."

"He made everything. Right?"

She studied the child a moment before she answered. "Everything and everyone."

Lindy excused herself and went to her room.

Gwen's gaze followed the child. "That's not like her."

"Maybe she's tired. It's been a long day." But Gwen was right. It wasn't like her.

They both pushed from the table and hurried after the child.

12

G wen paused at the doorway to Lindy's bedroom, Matt at her side. She couldn't let his presence distract her from concern over Lindy. The child had placed her collection of feathers in a spray on top of her dresser and one by one she picked them up and arranged them between her fingers. Done, she faced them.

"I have wings." She held out her arms with the feathers poking out from her fingers. "I'm a fowl of the air." She flapped her arms. "There's not 'nough room in here for a bird to fly." A scowl marked her sweet features.

Gwen looked to Matt, hoping he'd had a way of making Lindy see she would never be able to fly. His eyes begged her for the same thing.

They pulled her to sit between them on the bed.

Their arms crossed each others on the child's back. A jolt of something warm and sweet—and totally unfamiliar—filled Gwen from fingertip to toe. She tried to keep her gaze lowered, and avoid eye contact with him, but she was powerless to stop herself. Her eyes felt too big, too full of an emotion she couldn't control. *Please don't let him see anything but concern for Lindy.*

He looked directly at her. His eyes brimming with—

She lowered her eyes, uncertain of what she saw… what she hoped she saw…and then her gaze returned to him. Nothing existed apart from this moment. Full of unknown, beckoning possibilities.

Lindy shifted, piling feathers into her lap and Gwen turned her attention to the child. "Honey, why do you want to fly?" She understood it was in the hopes of finding her parents, but did Lindy understand her reasons?

Matt's arm pressed against hers, providing encouragement, yet also inviting her to soar. She shook her head. Was she getting as fanciful as Lindy?

"I just do." Lindy's words were half desperate, half stubborn.

"You run fast enough it's almost like flying." Gwen hoped her words would comfort the child.

"No, I don't."

"I have an idea." Matt waited for Lindy to give him her attention before he continued. "How would you like me to take you for a horseback ride? We could go so fast it would feel like you have wings."

Lindy bounced to her feet. Gwen's arm fell to the bed as did Matt's. Their fingers nestled together. The two becoming one. Gwen couldn't say who pulled back first. She clasped her hands tightly and ordered her insides to stop quivering.

"Will you?" Lindy rocked forward on her toes, like a bird ready to leave the ground behind. "When?"

"Is tomorrow soon enough?" Humor brimmed his words.

Pleasure filled Gwen, not only at Lindy's eagerness but with joy, sheer joy at sharing the care of this child with Matt, sharing his home, anticipating their marriage—

"When I wake up?" Lindy pressed for the earliest possible moment.

Matt glanced at Gwen and at the expression in his eyes she sucked in a breath and blinked. He turned away before she could analyze what she thought she saw...what she wanted to see. "How about after breakfast?"

Lindy considered his offer. Her shoulders sank. "Fine."

Matt and Gwen smiled at each other as Matt held out his hand to help Gwen to her feet then they followed Lindy from her room.

The three of them worked to clean up the kitchen and do the dishes. The chore was as pleasant as yesterday's picnic. All because they worked together in harmony. Matt teased Lindy making her laugh. He playfully flicked the tea towel at Gwen, never getting close enough to make her feel threatened. In turn, she dabbed a soapy drop of water on his nose.

He caught her wrist. Time froze as they faced each other. The only thing that moved was her frantic heartbeat, racing upward as if trying to fly free. Lindy put a fork in the drawer, the sound was a warning bell.

Gwen jerked back to the wash basin. What was wrong with her? Did she have a desire to embarrass herself? Yes, they would share the house, living side by side in it, when—if—they married. That didn't give her permission to dream of more. She scrubbed at the last dish, running the rag over and over the surface until Matt spoke softly.

"I think it's clean."

"Oh, right. I was lost in thought." Lost in mental scolding but wasn't that the same thing?

She handed him the item. She hadn't even realized it was a plate. While she emptied the water and put away the basin, Lindy prepared for bed and returned carrying two books to the settee. Her look informed Gwen that she expected them both to sit beside her and read. Telling herself they'd done this before did nothing to ease the tension gripping Gwen's spine yet somehow, she made her way across the room and sat beside Lindy as Matt sat on the other side of the child.

Somehow, she read aloud without her voice cracking. Somehow, she listened to Matt read without swallowing so loudly that she drew his attention. She rose to take Lindy to her room and tuck her in. Before she crossed the threshold, Matt was on his feet.

"It's been a long day. I'll say good night."

"Good night." She managed to stammer the word. He'd left in a hurry. Had he been aware of her inner turmoil and wanted to escape it? Her cheeks burned at the thought.

AFTER A GOOD NIGHT'S sleep and a long, serious talk with herself, Gwen was ready to face Matt the next morning when he came for breakfast. Lindy could barely contain her impatience over the promised ride.

"Are you done eating?" she asked Matt when he had a forkful of eggs halfway to his mouth.

"Mind if I finish my eggs and drink my coffee?" His humor-filled look at Gwen undid all the progress she'd made with her serious talk. Her heart strained at its moorings.

"She was up long before her regular time going from window to window."

"Well." Lindy crossed her arms and looked disgusted with the slow-moving, slow-eating adults. "I want to fly."

"Don't you mean ride?" Gwen reminded Lindy even though she knew it was one and the same for her.

Lindy didn't respond but sat watching Matt's every mouthful.

His gaze connected with Gwen's again, flashing with amusement. He scraped his plate clean and downed his coffee. "I'm done."

Lindy was on her feet and headed for the door before Matt could shove his chair back.

Chuckling, he followed her. "It looks like she's coming to supervise saddling the horse. Oh, by the way, could you pack a lunch for me? I won't be back at noon."

"Of course. No problem."

"Thanks for breakfast." The door closed quietly behind them.

Gwen hurried to the window to watch. Lindy raced ahead and waved at Matt to hurry. He glanced over his shoulder. Gwen couldn't say for certain if he saw her through the glass, but he gave a little salute and then trotted after Lindy.

* * *

MATT CLUNG to Lindy as they galloped down the road. She waved her arms and lifted her face to the wind like she wanted to take off into the air. They rode for two miles then he reined in and turned around.

"Aww, are we done?"

"'Fraid so. I've got work to do and Aunt Gwen will be wondering where we are."

"I like Auntie Gwen. Don't you?"

"Yup. I like her fine." Just fine.

Lindy shifted so she could look at Matt. "She's gonna stay forever, isn't she?"

"Forever is a long time."

Lindy's shoulders sank forward. "She might fly away like Mama and Papa."

"Oh, Lindy, I hope not." He'd told himself the delay in the wedding plans was to protect this little girl. Yet, she was all too aware that people could be snatched from one's life. Was there no way to shelter her?

The answer came so clearly. Hadn't Ma said they needed to trust God for the future? It was a hard lesson for a child to learn.

"Fly some more," Lindy said. Glad to oblige, they raced the last few yards going directly to his house. He carried her inside and set her down on the floor. She immediately flapped her arms. "I was almost flying."

The affection in Gwen's eyes as she watched the child lingered as she met Matt's gaze. He allowed himself to believe some of it might be for him.

"Your lunch is ready." She indicated the sack on the cupboard. "When will you be back?"

"I'm taking supplies to one of the line shacks. I should be back before dark. You don't need to hold supper for me." In the past, he might have spent the night away from home but not now. It wasn't fair to leave Gwen on her own that long. At least that was his reasoning and because he didn't intend to speak the words aloud, there was no one to argue the matter.

Luke had the pack horse loaded and ready to go when Matt reached the barn.

"I could go in your place," he offered.

"It's my turn, isn't it?" They had long ago set up a schedule for the task.

"Yeah but—"

"Then I'll be on my way." He took the lead rope of the pack animal. His travels required he cross Shannon Valley far to the north where the land leveled out and then cut to the west. He looked at the position of the sun in the sky. He was getting a late start. There was no way he could make it back before dark.

"Tell Gwen I won't be back tonight."

Luke rocked back on his heels. "My pleasure." His grin was wickedly teasing. The look in his eyes made Matt want to grind his teeth together.

"Don't forget she's mine."

"You neglected to put a ring on her finger. Guess that means I can do my best to convince her she'd be making a mistake to marry you when I'm available."

"You wouldn't dare," Matt growled the words.

Luke's reply was a mocking laugh.

Although he knew Luke was teasing, trying to get a rise out of him, he reined down the trail. "Never mind. I'll tell her myself. And you leave her alone." He went to the house and informed Gwen he wouldn't be back until tomorrow.

"Oh." A whole lot of disappointment laced that little word. "Well, have a good trip."

"Thanks, and you have a good day." He returned to the horse and continued toward his destination.

Seemed like she might miss him.

13

*L*aundry flapped on the line. Gwen had certainly not gotten it done before breakfast, but she didn't mind. It gave her something to do to pass the long hours. She hadn't planted the rose bush Opal had brought her, either. To do so signified she knew she'd be staying. She smiled as she dug a spot for it under the kitchen window.

She put the bush into the hole and packed dirt around it. The idea of a marriage in name only didn't sound as appealing as it had when she first arrived, but it guaranteed her a home. And a permanent place in Matt's life. That was enough for her. It had to be.

Lindy darted in and out of Gwen's presence. There was something about the child today that made Gwen sit back on her heels to watch her. Perhaps she was sorrowful and didn't know how to deal with her feelings.

Gwen made up her mind. "Let's have a picnic lunch." She watered the newly-planted bush.

Lindy skidded to a halt. "Can we go down to the valley?"

"I promised I wouldn't go without Matt." Or one of the other men but she couldn't imagine going with anyone else.

"Oh." Lindy's shoulders sank.

"I think you might have other favorite places to go."

Lindy considered the words for a moment. "You wanna have a picnic in the loft with the cats?"

The loft? Gwen shuddered. "Wouldn't you prefer being in the sunshine?" She lifted her face to the sky. "It's such a nice day. We could go back to the table in the clearing." She hoped Lindy would choose something... anything but the loft.

"Can we go past Uncle Luke's house?"

The child had been forbidden to go beyond on her own, but they could go together. She was curious to see more. "That sounds like fun. Give me time to clean up and make a lunch."

The laundry wasn't dry yet so Gwen could leave with a clear conscience, and she packed food for them both.

They passed Luke's house and the place where the trail divided; one side leading to the valley floor. They stayed on the other branch. Lindy skipped ahead with all the assurance of having been this way before. After a bit of running and flapping her arms, Lindy fell back to walk by Gwen.

She chattered like a magpie as they continued on their way. Why was the sky blue? Do birds ever fall from the sky? Had Gwen ever seen a baby horse born? Lindy had once with her pa. Would Lindy have to leave when she grew up?

Gwen chuckled. "You might fall in love and marry someone and be willing to go wherever he wanted."

Lindy shook her head. "No, I won't." She ground to a halt to stare at Gwen. "Are you sad to be here? You know, 'cause you had to leave your before home."

Gwen scooped up the child, hugged her, and kissed her neck. "If I hadn't left my previous home, I would never have met you. So how can I be sad?" It was true. She no longer held any regret about leaving Kellom. Patricia had been unkind about persuading Gwen to go but she'd been right. There was nothing for her back there. She released Lindy to run ahead. Here her future glowed with joy.

They found a grassy spot for their picnic that gave Gwen a view north to green hills. The mountains glistened to the west. They giggled together at a ladybug climbing a stalk of grass. And at a flock of blackbirds flying overhead.

As they returned home Gwen thought how pleasant it had been to spend the afternoon in the company of a sweet child. Only one thing was missing to make her joy complete, but she would not admit what it was.

The rest of the day passed quickly enough with bringing in the laundry, folding and putting some away, and rolling the rest to be ironed. She made a simple supper for herself and Lindy.

After she'd tucked Lindy in, Gwen circled the sitting room, deciding where she would hang the few pictures she'd brought with her, thinking how she might use some of her savings to buy a rug to warm the room during the winter months. She'd brought doilies and knickknacks and got them from her trunk. Soon the room had a more welcoming feel to it.

She sat in the rocker to read her Bible and pray for Matt's safety. Finally, admitting there was no point in staying up all night, she went to her bed.

It had been a long day, but sleep did not come easily. How could she miss him when he'd never slept in the house since her arrival? And yet she did.

THE NEXT MORNING, she created a mental list of things to do in order to keep busy. Ironing. Weeding the garden. Preserving rhubarb for the winter. She encouraged Lindy to help as much as possible which made many tasks take longer but kept them both happily active.

It was late afternoon, jars of ruby-red rhubarb

cooled on the cupboard when Lindy hollered. "Uncle Matt's back."

Gwen wiped her hands and ducked into her bedroom to check her hair. Her fingers lingered on the pins. Should she let it down? No, of course not. It would simply be in the way. He'd go to the barn and take care of the animals before he came to the house. Thankfully, she'd prepared supper in preparation for his return.

She hurriedly wiped the table clean and was about to grab plates to set it when she heard his boots on the outer step. Her breath caught midway down and refused to budge any further. She stared at the entrance, her hands clenched in front of her.

He came through the door, his head bare, a ring around his dark hair from his hat. His gaze met hers. The air grew warm and sweet. He smiled.

Suddenly she was freed of her inertia. "Welcome home." She hoped her voice didn't sound as husky to him as it did to her.

He stepped forward until he was within reach. "I got back as fast as I could." His words promised a world of blessing. "It sure smells good in here."

Her lungs deflated. Of course, he was glad to be home and have a meal waiting for him. "It's about ready. Sit down and I'll pour you some coffee." She'd put it to brew when Lindy announced his return. She filled a cup for him and then set the table, her hands moving automatically.

Lindy sat at her place and regaled him with stories of what they'd done.

The little girl was in bed before the adults got a chance to talk.

"The cabin has been damaged in a storm, so I have to return in the morning with material to repair it. I'll be away two, more likely, three days."

Did he sound regretful? About having to leave again? Don't be silly. It was because of the storm damage.

"That's too bad." She hoped he would think the sadness in her tone was about the cabin.

"Will you be all right on your own?"

On her own? "Is everyone going?"

"Oh, no, sorry. I didn't mean to alarm you. Luke and I are the only ones. Wally will be home every evening. I'm not sure about Andy and Riley. They might be here or not."

"I'll be fine on my own. Lindy and I have been enjoying ourselves. I've found things to keep me busy." She nodded toward the jars of rhubarb.

"We'll be away early tomorrow."

"I'll make breakfast before you go." Maybe they'd linger at the table for a few minutes, taking pleasure in each other's company.

"Gwen, we'll leave as soon as it's light enough to see the trail. You stay in bed and relax."

She nodded though she couldn't deny a twinge of dismissal. Of course, he didn't need her to see him off.

Or to feed him breakfast. She was here to take care of Lindy and she would be doing exactly that.

She heard horses leaving the next morning. She jumped from the bed and hurried to the window to watch them depart. With slow feet, she returned to crawl under the covers and lie staring at the shifting light on the ceiling. *Two, more likely, three days.* Forty-eight or maybe seventy-two hours. They stretched out before her like an endless road.

She'd go visit Opal, but Matt had never again given her a lesson in driving the wagon. She certainly wasn't about to try it on her own even if she could find someone to harness the horses.

If only the garden was farther along, she could put up vegetables for the winter. *Enough of feeling sorry for myself.* She'd never been one for such behavior and got from her bed, dressed, and went to the kitchen to prepare breakfast for herself and Lindy.

After the meal, Lindy asked, "Can I get the rest of my stuff?"

Gwen's hands stilled in the dishwater. "You mean from the big house?"

"Yup."

"That sounds like a good idea." As soon as the last dish was dried and in the cupboard, Gwen got two valises from her bedroom and they went to the house. Gwen knocked but no one answered.

"Go on in," Wally called. "Andy's gone for the day."

Gwen followed Lindy to her room where the child started pulling clothes from drawers.

"Hang on a minute, missy. Let's do it neatly." Gwen opened the valises and arranged the clothing and toys inside. There were a few books on the shelf and Lindy said she'd take those. Finally, the room was empty of her belongings, and they returned to their house and spent an hour arranging everything to Lindy's satisfaction.

Over the next two days, they established a routine of sorts. Baking and mending, weeding the garden, and picnics outside. In the evening, while Lindy slept, Gwen wrote to Maurice, Mrs. Strong, and a few friends. When Matt hadn't returned the second night, Gwen consoled herself that he would arrive the next day.

Unless they'd encountered some other problem. But she couldn't let herself think along those lines.

* * *

"Can't these pack horses go any faster?" Matt tugged at the lead rope.

Luke roared with laughter. "Anxious to get home, are ya? Can't say as I blame you. She's worth rushing home to."

"How would you know that?" Matt was a tad grouchy after more than two days of Luke's teasing.

No way would he admit it was because he was missing his home. His *home*, mind you. Not the people in it.

That didn't sound right. Sure, he missed them too. More than he cared to confess.

"Uh oh."

Matt jerked his attention to Luke. "Look at the sky over the mountains."

Uh oh was right. Black clouds foamed and boiled.

"We're in for a soaking if we don't get a move on."

Luke agreed. Together they urged the pack animals to a faster pace. They were making good time as the clouds rolled closer, forcing them to gallop the last half mile.

Matt leaped off his horse and unsaddled the animals in seconds, Luke taking a more leisurely pace. Matt hung the last bridle on the wall and trotted from the barn, ignoring Luke's mocking laugh. He didn't slow down until he reached the house and burst inside.

"I just made it." The door sucked shut with a bang.

Gwen glanced up. "Look what the wind blew in."

"Do you see the storm coming?" He crossed the room and beckoned her to join him at the window.

The mountains had disappeared in heavy clouds. The valley was obscured by mist. A strong gust of wind hit them. Rain drove into the window, rattling the glass.

Gwen leaned forward as if to see better. "It's amazing."

"It doesn't frighten you?" Surprise edged his words.

"Not in the least. We're all safely indoors and together. The house is warm and dry. What's to be frightened of?"

Her smile flooded her eyes and drove away the chill of the approaching storm. They lingered side by side. In order for them both to see the view, they had to stand with their shoulders pressed together. Never mind that the only thing they could see was rain slashing across the glass.

Her arm was warm against his. Their breathing synchronized. A sense of contentment filled his heart. Having her here was right and good.

Lindy ducked in front of them to look out. "Can't see nothin'." Her tone indicated she thought they had something wrong with them to stare at a rain-streaked window.

Gwen hurried to the stove. "Would you like coffee and cookies? It's too early for supper. Besides, it isn't ready yet. The roast won't be done, and I still have to prepare potatoes."

"Coffee sounds great. Thanks." He parked himself at the table as she set out a cup and a plate of cookies. "Only one cup?" He quirked an eyebrow.

"I need to finish meal preparations. You go ahead and enjoy."

Lindy sidled up to him. "I helped Auntie Gwen make the cookies. Do you like them?"

He hugged the little girl to his side. "Best I ever tasted." But his gaze was on Gwen.

She fussed with something on the cupboard.

What was wrong with him? Didn't he remember their agreement? Even more than that, had he forgotten how much it hurt to allow himself feelings for a woman? He forced his mind back to that day waiting at the train depot. His heart had been ripped from his chest. He'd left it bleeding on the wooden platform.

Only it had found its way back to his body. And waited to be recognized.

He downed scalding hot coffee and followed it with a cookie that he didn't even taste. Only a foolish man would venture into a mine pit knowing the risk of explosions and he was not a foolish man.

He turned his mind to the story Lindy was telling him of how she'd spent the days when Matt had been away. Suddenly, she said something that captured his attention.

"I brung my things over here."

"From the other house?" He looked at Gwen for clarification.

She nodded, warmth in her eyes. "It was her idea. Everything is in her room." She tipped her head in that direction.

He hugged the child to his side again. "That's good." Something satisfying passed between himself and

Gwen. Acknowledgment of Lindy's acceptance of the changes in her life.

"I think I owe this to you." His voice was husky as he spoke to Gwen.

Her smile settled nicely into his heart. Perhaps that was all he needed—some sort of acknowledgment.

"It's no more my doing than yours." Her gaze darted away as if checking on something on the stove. But he sensed her withdrawal as she continued, her voice steady. "If you hadn't been willing to seek a mail-order bride and if you hadn't offered me the position and if I…" Her words trailed off.

If she hadn't agreed to accept his condition. A marriage in name only.

He stared at the bottom of his empty coffee cup. "It was a good decision." He stole a glance at her, hoping his words had reassured her that he wasn't about to demand a different agreement, but her back was to him as she prepared food.

Lindy tugged his hand. "Come, see my room." She opened each drawer and showed him the contents. One had been reserved for her collection of feathers and rocks, a few books, and an old ball. It had once been Roscoe's. He and Matt had played many games with it.

His throat tightened at the memories.

"Auntie Gwen made a bed for my dolly." Lindy showed him.

Gwen had fashioned a basket into a crib for the

doll Lindy had gotten for Christmas last year. Merry had been thrilled to get her daughter one with a real China face but had warned Lindy that she must be careful with the fragile toy.

Lindy tucked the blanket more securely around the doll. "She likes it here."

"That's good."

Lindy had stories about the doll, the books on the shelf, and various other things. Matt listened to her happy chatter. "You're very imaginative."

"That's what Auntie Gwen said. And she said it was a good thing."

"Yes, it is."

Lindy stopped in front of him and studied him hard. He waited to see what she wanted.

"Auntie Gwen is staying, isn't she? You'll make sure, won't you?"

His heart clenched so hard that his muscles twitched. Had she suggested otherwise to Lindy? "I believe she is."

"Uncle Andy says she doesn't have to unless you marry her." Two little fists bunched to her hips. "He says you ought to marry her right now. Why don'cha? Why don't you make sure she doesn't fly away?"

He tried for humor even though he felt none inside. "Well, little gal, in case you didn't notice, it's raining like a waterfall out there. I think she'd prefer to stay here where it's warm and dry."

Lindy huffed and stalked from the room.

He asked himself the same question as he followed her from the room. Why didn't he suggest they marry right away? She'd certainly proven to be efficient, kind, and someone he liked having around.

"Supper is ready," Gwen announced.

They gathered around the table, enjoying thick slices of bread and a savory stew while outside, the wind blew, and the rain fell.

After the kitchen was clean, they settled in together in the front room. Lindy brought out some of her rocks and feathers and arranged them to her liking. Gwen had a basket of sewing in her lap and examined several pieces. Matt wondered what she meant to make with them.

He had some older newspapers with items he had yet to read. They seemed very far removed from the harsh elements even though the storm bellowed and raged outdoors. The evening passed and they put Lindy to bed. She still hadn't invited him to go with her to say good night.

He should leave now but the rain still battered the little house and he wanted to say he had changed his mind about delaying the wedding. Mentally, he rehearsed how he would word the request.

Gwen returned and looked at the storm-darkened window. "Stay a little longer. Perhaps it will let up."

"Very well." He watched her cut and stitch pink fabric and the shape of a doll's body emerged. His thoughts, however, were not on her project but on his.

He was about to break the silence with his request to marry sooner when she looked up, mistaking his steady gaze for interest.

"I'm making a doll for Lindy. One she can drag around and play with." She held up the unfinished product to show him. "I have made dolls for some time now. In fact—" She lowered her gaze to the doll then darted a glance at him. "I had a reputation for out-of-the-ordinary dolls."

He studied the item in her hands. "I can see why already. The features almost look real."

She gave a soft, self-deprecating sigh. "That's my goal." She grew serious. "Each of these is like my own baby." Her gaze raised to him. "My only babies."

He blinked, taking in the intensity of her look. Dark eyes that seemed to open to her very soul. He was being sucked in, feeling the depth of her sorrow as she acknowledged the pain of knowing their agreement meant she would never have any other child but Lindy.

What would she say if he suggested they changed the terms of that agreement? Surely it wouldn't hurt to ask that as well.

"Gwen, about—"

A flash of lightning seared his eyes. A roar of thunder followed in the same second. Before the second clap thundered, they were both on their feet, Gwen in his arms. And then a second and third thunder came, shaking the house. They clung to each other as the sound rolled and rumbled.

There was a short interval before the next streak of lightning came, illuminating her features in silver. She cringed against him when the thunder followed. He held her to his chest, his heart beating in time with hers, jolting with each clap of thunder.

The noise of the storm lessened. Or did he block it out as he studied her upturned face, her eyes too large, her lips parted. As he watched, her look went from alarm to something else that he dared to call aware-ness. She trailed her gaze over his face and back to his eyes. He lost himself for a moment in the tiny dimple in her left cheek, a sweet reminder of her happiness. Her lips drew his attention, and he couldn't pull away. His arms encircled her even as she wrapped hers around his waist, clinging to him.

"Gwen." He lowered his head.

Someone banged on the door and threw it open before they could spring apart or call for the visitor to enter.

14

Heat stung Gwen's cheeks. She wasn't normally frightened by thunder and lightning but to have it occur simultaneously was a different matter...something she'd never experienced before. Her scalp had tingled. The smell of gunpowder had filled the air, and she'd fled to Matt's arms for shelter.

Only fear had given way to something else... awareness of him as more than a protector. More than a man she planned to share a home with. Her heart had beat an incessant demand. She wanted more than his name. More than his home. More than his protection.

As her gaze searched his, she admitted she would have welcomed a kiss. Unfortunately, the banging door interrupted the moment.

Luke stood in the doorway. "Riley's house has been struck. Come on, we have to see what the damage is."

"Coming." Matt paused to speak to Gwen. "Will you be all right on your own?"

"Of course." Her words came out strong and confident—in total opposition to the trembling of her insides.

"I'll be back to let you know how things are." The door of the entryway clicked. They were gone.

She heard nothing more but the storm. Inside her, raged a storm of another sort. She'd agreed to marriage in name only, but she was finding it difficult, if not impossible not to want more. He'd not once suggested he might be willing to change his mind. What if she proposed they adjust the terms of their agreement? But would it give Matt reason to reject her?

Pain slashed through her at the possibility. She'd come wanting nothing but a permanent home. And perhaps, appreciation for her abilities. But the yawning ache inside her caused her to wonder if that would be enough. She wouldn't put her future at risk by confessing her feelings.

Determined to put her restless thoughts aside, she went to the window to watch and wait for the man she wanted to marry.

Lightning glazed the scene in silver for seconds. Not long enough to make out any details. And then darkness reigned. No flames leaped from Riley's house. Was it even possible for anything to burn in this deluge?

She wandered from window to window, staring into the storm. She took the lamp to Lindy's room and held it high to assure herself the little girl was asleep. Back in the sitting room, she picked up her sewing basket but the doll she'd begun no longer held her interest and she returned the container to her bedroom.

The minutes turned into hours. Were the men safe? She sank to the rocking chair and prayed for them.

A rattle at the door jerked her awake. Her hand pressed to her throat. She hadn't meant to sleep while Matt was fighting the storm and she pushed to her feet and stumbled to the entryway.

He stood on the kitchen floor, dripping wet and shivering. "There was some damage to Riley's house and one of the storage sheds, but we got both holes patched." His teeth rattled from the cold.

"You're freezing." She pulled him toward the stove.

"I'm going to get the floor wet."

"It will dry. Here, take off your coat." She tugged at the sleeves. His hands were like blocks of ice. "Sit down and I'll pull your boots off." She dragged a chair closer, and he sank to it.

She tugged at the boots, but they stuck. She leaned into the task and pulled until they finally left his feet. "Do you have dry clothes in your bedroom?" She knew he did because she'd been in there to dust. "Go and change while I make something warm for you to drink."

He went to his room. She could imagine the wet items puddling on the floor as she made tea and laced it with honey. Maybe more honey than she'd planned as her thoughts seemed stuck in his room.

He returned, his teeth chattering.

She touched his cheek, welcoming the excuse for physical contact. Chills raced down her spine at how cold he was. "You're like ice. Sit by the fire." She grabbed the quilt from his bed and brought it back to drape over him.

"Thank you." His eyes caught hers, dark as the sky outside, but so alive and warm. Like embers of a fire burning away what little determination she had stored up. Tension filled the room, pushing into her lungs until she could only get in tiny bits of air.

She was drawn to him like a moth to lamp light. Ready for the flames. Welcoming them. She leaned closer.

He blinked. The fire died. It had only been her imagination. She pretended her only reason for being almost nose-to-nose with him was to draw the quilt around his shoulders. Her hands empty, her heart thudding heavily, she stepped back.

Remembering she'd prepared him a hot drink, she placed the cup in his hands and then forced her quivering legs to his room to retrieve the wet clothing from the floor. She hung it over the washtub where the water could drip all night. Cold drops rattled against the tin. A mocking sound that echoed inside her head. Splat. Love. Splat. Not. Splat. Part of the agreement. Sploosh. Each sound, each thought burned its memory into her head. She pressed her lips together, gathered her thoughts into a bundle, and tucked them into a dark corner of her mind willing them to stay out of sight. A marriage of convenience was better than nothing. It gave her almost all she wanted—security and permanency. No one needed to know that she loved Matt.

When she returned, she stood close to him as if she could spread her warmth to his body. As if he'd feel her emotions by osmosis and welcome them even as he welcomed physical warmth.

He pulled a chair closer. "You make me nervous with your hovering. Sit down and keep me company."

She tried to smile but her lips refused to cooperate. "I'm worried about you. What if you get pneumonia?" Worry was but one of the feelings worming through her thoughts, but it was the only one she would confess.

"I won't. I've been wetter and colder before." His gaze blazed with warmth. "But never better taken care of."

Somewhat mollified, she sank into the chair. Their knees almost touched, and she felt the cold wafting from him. She shivered. Not from cold but from the other things racing through her veins that upset her equilibrium. Fear of losing her home if he guessed how she felt. Uncertainty…would he find her acceptable as a wife? Futile wishes. She wanted it all. Marriage, home, and love.

Again, she dismissed the wayward thoughts. Again, she pushed them away wishing them out of her head. What she had promised, she would do. No one would accuse her of being fickle.

A knock sounded on the door. Gwen's heart kicked against her ribs. Surely Matt wouldn't need to go out in the rain again.

Andy stepped inside without waiting for an answer. He eyed the two of them. "Cozy."

Gwen would have gotten to her feet but didn't want to give Andy the idea she felt guilty when she didn't and had no reason to. They were simply sitting by the stove.

Andy's hard gaze rested on his brother. "I brought a slicker so you'd keep dry on the way back to my house."

Back to the other house? His words vibrated through Gwen. "It's still storming."

Rain and wind battered the house. What if the storm intensified? She didn't care for the idea of being alone should they again experience such close lightning. Matt rose, letting the quilt fall to the chair.

She grabbed his arm. "I don't want to be on my own."

He covered her hand with his. At least there was

warmth in his touch now, not the iciness of a few minutes ago. Or was it hours? She couldn't keep time straight in her head.

He squeezed her hand. "I'll stay." The words were a blessing, a promise, a—.

She wouldn't allow her thoughts to go further.

Matt and Andy studied each other from their positions across the room.

"I'm staying." Matt's voice was low, but his tone clearly said he wasn't about to change his mind. "And in the morning, we'll ride to town, and get married." He turned to Gwen. "If that meets your approval?"

"It does." Her words held conviction as her heart gave a happy thump.

Andy lifted a hand. "Fine by me." The door closed quietly behind him.

Matt's gaze had not left Gwen's. Nor could she look away. He was ready to marry her. She'd met his approval. This house would be her home. Only one thing was missing. A home for her heart with him.

A thud against the house startled Gwen. She jerked her hands to her throat as her heart beat an answering thud.

"Just something blowing against the wall," Matt said. He shoved his hands in his pockets and shifted restlessly as if looking for an escape from where he stood. "I suppose we should try and get some sleep." He waited for her response.

She nodded, feeling dismissed, and went toward her room.

"Good night, Gwen."

"Good night, Matt."

"Call if you need anything."

"I will." *I need you to love me.* She walked calmly to her room even though a storm raged in her heart.

She quickly prepared for bed and slid under the covers. He'd offered her marriage and a home. He'd moved up the date for the wedding to tomorrow. When she came west, she'd believed it all she needed or wanted was security, acceptance, and perhaps approval. Someone who valued her enough to keep her in his life. Unlike Kenny or Wilson who had no trouble walking away from her without concern for her feelings. Or Maurice who barely shrugged at her departure.

JOY SWELLED in her heart the next morning. Sun shone through the window. The storm had passed, and diamonds sparkled on every leaf and blade of glass. Puddles dotted the trail.

Today was her wedding day. She had a dress she'd saved for the occasion. It wasn't a typical bridal gown. She'd chosen something more practical—a gray silk taffeta that rustled like a whisper when she moved in it. The dress had been specially made for her for Maurice's wedding, the only time she'd worn it. She brushed her hand over the skirt. Today they would get married.

She hugged herself and slipped into her regular cotton dress. No one had said when they would leave for town. In the meantime, they needed breakfast, so she left her room to get started. Matt stepped from his room into the living area at the same time, his hair rumpled.

"Good morning." Her voice carried the music of her heart.

He smiled. "And to you."

Lindy trotted from her room and skidded to a halt as her gaze went from Gwen to Matt. "You stayed with us." Her voice filled with awe then she darted to the window. "Storm's over. Everything's wet."

Gwen hurried to the kitchen to put the coffee on the stove. "I'll whip up something in a minute." She'd fry the cooked potatoes she had, add some eggs, and slice bread.

In a few minutes, they were around the table, food on their plates and coffee in the adults' cups. Matt offered a quick prayer of gratitude for safety in the storm.

It was nothing different than they'd done from the first and yet the air shimmered with promise.

They'd almost finished the meal when Riley burst into the room without knocking. "One of the cowhands just rode in. The cattle have stampeded. Goodness knows where they are. All hands are needed to round them up. Saddle up. Let's go." Riley waved at Matt to come along then dashed out the door.

"I'm sorry." Matt pushed from the table and slowly got to his feet. "Our plans will have to wait."

"That's fine." It wasn't as if she'd always planned to get married today. No, she'd planned to marry upon her arrival.

"I don't know how long this will take. I don't like to leave you on your own."

His concern warmed her insides. "Will anyone be staying at the ranch besides Lindy and me?"

"I doubt it. Like Riley said, all hands are needed." He got as far as the door and waited. She couldn't guess why. Did he want more than a goodbye? Or was that her own wish making itself known?

"Goodbye," she said. "I hope everything goes well."

Lindy rushed over and hugged Matt. "Goodbye. See you soon."

THE DAYS PASSED with sullen slowness. One. Two. Three. On the fourth day she stopped counting. That afternoon someone rode into the yard. The rider didn't stop at any of the houses but went to a supply shed.

Gwen and Lindy trotted over to investigate. Wally hurried to load a pack animal with sacks of beans, rice, cornmeal, and canned goods. He paused long enough to greet them.

"It's turned into quite a job." He added more items to his load. "We was just about finished when something spooked them and we have to start all over. Cows can be unpredictable critters."

"How much longer will it take?"

"No telling for certain. There's many places them cows can hide." He rubbed his chin. "But I'd say at least three more days. Give or take." He secured the ropes on the pack and prepared to remount.

"How is everyone?" What she really meant was how is Matt?

"Riding every daylight hour and more. I gotta go. Bye, miss. I'll tell Matt you asked after him."

"But I didn't." Her words were lost in the clop of departing hooves.

Lindy took her hand and together they returned to the house. Gwen tried to keep busy, tried to keep her mind occupied, but she'd never felt so alone. If not for Lindy, she might have given in to her loneliness and walked to town. How absurd. It would be a very long walk.

There was only so much baking one could do when only she and Lindy were there to eat it. She worked on the doll in the evenings, finding enjoyment in the task. She read her Bible and prayed for Matt and the men out among the cows. At least Lindy seemed happy enough. She often disappeared but always came when Gwen called.

"Lindy," she called her for lunch. When she heard

no response, she called again and waited. After several minutes the child trotted down the path toward Gwen. "Where were you?"

"Playing with the kittens. You should see them. They's getting so big."

She'd love to see them but not if it meant going up to the loft. "You're spending a lot of time with them."

"Yup." She skipped ahead to the house and sat at the table.

As time dragged by, Gwen began going to where the trail drew close to the valley and staring out, hoping for some sign of the men returning, or even of Matt coming back on his own.

But not once did she see anyone. Today was no different although she'd stood there for an hour squinting into the distance. Right after breakfast, she'd baked a lardie cake in the hopes he'd return and enjoy the surprise.

With a sigh that came from the depths of her being, she returned to the house to make lunch. A little later, she called Lindy and waited. Then moved down the trail toward the barn and called again. And again. Lindy must be too busy playing to hear her. She went to the barn door and called.

"Lindy." When the child didn't answer, Gwen forced herself to climb the ladder until she could see into the loft. "Lindy?" No sign of the child.

She returned to ground level and left the barn. Calling Lindy, she searched the garden, the little clearing, and around each house. She went into Andy's house, calling as she looked through the place. No little girl. She even checked every bed in case Lindy had fallen asleep on one of them.

There was still Wally's house and she forced herself to go in the neat, three-bedroom cabin. But no child. Had she gone into one of the other houses and hadn't heard Gwen call? A quick search of each revealed no missing child.

Gwen stood in the yard and hollered her name over and over.

No need to worry, she soothed herself. Lindy often got preoccupied. But after another search and enough calling to make her throat hurt, she retraced her steps in case they had crossed paths somewhere.

Nothing. Her breath caught on her parched tongue. Had she lost the child? Taking care of her was the only reason she was here. She must find Lindy. *Please, God. Help me. Let her be safe.*

She broke into a run. Her heart and lungs stalled as she raced by Luke's house to the trail leading down to the valley floor. What if she'd gone down the forbidden path. Gwen wiped the sweat from her eyes and studied the ground. No evidence of a small-sized shoe. She squinted and forced herself to breathe slowly so she could scan the valley floor. There was no telltale movement below.

Where was she? A sob clawed up her throat. She

couldn't fail. Not now. Not when she wanted to stay here more than anything else.

Gwen circled the buildings again. By the time she'd searched each one her stomach knotted like an old rope. Nausea grabbed at her throat. She choked it back. No time for that.

She grabbed her skirts to keep from tripping on them and ran down the road hoping to see a little girl trudging in the dust.

Nothing. She stood in the middle of the yard, alone. Where, oh where was Lindy?

15

Matt was tired and dirty as he and his brothers headed home. He'd never put in more wearying days. Chasing cows who didn't want to be chased any more than Matt wanted to chase them. He wanted to be home. Or more accurately, taking Gwen to town so they could get married. For the next mile, his fatigue was forgotten amidst the plans forming in his head. He'd take her to the church, promise her forever. He'd protect her and Lindy, ensuring a future full of love and bliss.

A faint bell tinkled in the background of his thoughts. A reminder of his helplessness to prevent a train accident, a wagon accident, illness, and…

The ranch buildings were in sight, and he urged his horse to a gallop, his troublesome thoughts dismissed.

Gwen ran toward the barn as they rode in.

Luke chuckled. "Someone's glad to see you."

Matt managed not to grin his pleasure.

Gwen skidded to a halt before them. "I can't find Lindy." Her face was flushed and sweaty, her hair escaping from the bun she wore.

"What do you mean?" The words were harsher than he meant but why was she upset? Lindy knew every inch of the yard.

"She's disappeared. I've looked everywhere. For hours." She hurried on, her words hot bullets searing a burning trail through his formerly pleasant thoughts. "I searched the houses, the loft, up and down the trails, every building, every little clearing where she likes to play. I can't find her." She ended on a wail.

Gwen's concern was genuine even though Matt wasn't truly worried. This was an opportunity to prove he could protect those he loved, starting with Gwen. Dropping to the ground, he swept her into his arms. "We'll find her. She can't have gone far." Her shudders reverberated in his chest. He felt her desperation in the way she collapsed against him. As if she counted on him to take care of her concerns.

He would not fail. Not this time. Only one thing kept him from holding her until her shaking subsided... he must find Lindy and ease Gwen's worry.

He eased from the embrace. He would like to kiss away her tears but not now. He patted her arms and then swung into his saddle. "Fan out," he called to the others. The five of them circled the yard in ever-widening sweeps. Not finding her, they spread out more.

"I'll check the valley," he called, riding in that direction even though he was convinced she wouldn't have gone that way. She'd been thoroughly warned. He rubbed at the knot in his neck. If she had...

He couldn't quite convince himself it wasn't possible. Every muscle in his body clenched. There were so many dangers. Water. Risk of falling. Wild animals— he stopped. He'd find her safe and sound, singing one of her little tunes, and wonder why he'd been so anxious.

He crisscrossed the floor of the valley several times, checked the ground for footprints, peered into bushes, and rode under trees. Finally, convinced she wasn't there, he rode back up the trail to rejoin the others. One of them would have found her by now. But Riley and Wally sat on their horses, faces lined with worry.

Matt didn't need anyone to speak to know Lindy was still missing. He looked around for the other brothers.

Luke came up the road and sang out a hello drawing everyone's attention his way. "I've found her." He rode to Gwen and lowered the child to the ground.

Relief flowing through his veins, Matt dropped from the saddle and rushed to join them.

Gwen pulled Lindy into her arms and hugged her

tight. "Where were you?" She looked to Luke for the answer.

"She was down the trail, in a tree. I almost missed her, but my horse perked up his ears and I knew someone or something was there. It seems she climbed up the tree and then was too scared to get down." He lowered his voice. "Maybe a little afraid she'd be in trouble."

"I thought I could fly." Lindy's words came on a fractured breath. "But I can't."

Gwen hugged her again, holding her like she'd didn't want to ever let her go. "Honey, remember the angels in your book? They're the only ones who can fly."

Lindy hung her head. "I thought…"

"I know. You want to fly up to see your mama and papa, but it isn't time."

Matt squatted down to hug Lindy and found himself nudged aside as Andy wanted to hug her too. Then Wally and Riley.

The child was safe. That was all that mattered. That and Gwen. Matt needed to reassure her. Promise her they would always be safe in his care. But could he promise that? Life was so uncertain. Things so easily went wrong.

But before he could think what he wanted to speak, she lifted her skirt and fled to the house.

He took a step after her and then changed his mind. His thoughts were in turmoil, still jittery after the scare Lindy had given them. He ground around and strode to the barn, climbed to the loft, and sank to the floor with Cat and her kittens purring around him. He pulled the gray kitten to his lap and stroked it.

Every breath was a struggle as he faced the truth of his inadequacies, his failures. He hadn't been able to protect Corine. Hadn't been able to keep Ma from getting sick. Hadn't even been able to save the colt he'd raised by hand...something he hadn't thought of in a long time.

Loving meant having his heart ripped to shreds when he failed. When he had to stand by when things were out of his control. All he wanted was to protect those he loved. He pressed his fist to his chest. At the same time, protect his heart.

The kitten crawled from his lap and joined its litter mates nursing at their mother.

Cats had it easy. They were born, accepted the affection they were offered, and didn't worry about the future.

A truth slammed into his ribs. Cat enjoyed life because she had confidence that her humans would feed her and give her attention. Matt had someone more sufficient than a person. He had God. He was loved by God and protected by Him. His life was in hands so much bigger and stronger than his own that he needed to stop thinking he had to control everything.

Love might be risky. It might mean pain. But with

God holding their lives, he could face the future with confidence. He could give his heart wholly and freely to Gwen if she'd have it.

He bolted to his feet, slid down the ladder without using the rungs, and trotted across the yard. He needed to talk to Gwen, tell her he wanted to marry her, not only as a mother for Lindy, but because he loved her and couldn't imagine the future without her. No matter what the risks.

* * *

GWEN GRABBED the back of the chair, facing Matt as he rushed through the door. He skidded to a stop. She sucked in endless air that did nothing to calm her inner turmoil.

"I've something I want to say to you." His breathless words indicated he'd been running.

She held up her hand. "Please, let me go first." The ragged pounding in her head increased. The frightening hours of Lindy's disappearance had given Gwen plenty of opportunity to face her failings. And come to a decision.

"I've failed." She forced the words out. Each syllable scraped across her tongue. "I'm not what you need. You did right to ask for a delay in the wedding." Her insides were so tight, so painful she had to pause and wait for them to settle.

"Gwen—" He took a step toward her.

She pushed her hand toward him. If he came too close, she wouldn't be able to say what she must.

"You wanted someone who could keep Lindy safe. I've proven I can't."

He rocked his head back and forth and opened his mouth, but she rushed on before he could speak.

"You need to find someone else." The words revealed very little of the tremors that consumed her insides. She swallowed back rising nausea. She'd meant to prove herself necessary, invaluable, wanted... instead, she'd proven the opposite.

He leaned back on his heels. "I don't want you to leave."

"I...I..." The air whooshed from her lungs, and she couldn't finish. She didn't want to go but... "What value am I to you or Lindy?"

"Gwen." Her name sounded warm and cherished on his lips.

Her breath stalled somewhere between her lungs and hope as he closed the distance between them in slow strides.

The chair barred his approach. He gently lifted her hands from its back and set it aside. "Gwen, can I tell you what you are to me? You are everything I need and want. You are my spring and summer. The sunshine on a cloudy day. You fill my days with joy." His voice was so soft it sent shivers down her spine. He caught her by the shoulders, sending the shivers deeper, into the very core of her being. "You do the same for Lindy. More than that, you make me willing to accept the uncertainty of a future neither of us can control. I'm choosing to trust God instead." His voice deepened, echoing in her heart. "Gwen, what I'm trying to say is I love you. I want you to be in my life for now and always."

"You do?" He loved her. Valued her. Wanted her.

He waited, uncertainty in his expression.

She had failed but he still wanted her. It was beyond her wildest hope. Seeing uncertainty in his gaze, she let words flow from her heart. "Matt, I love you. Together, we can face the future."

He lowered his head and caught her mouth in a kiss full of tenderness.

Her heart was safe with him. And she'd hold his gently as long as she lived.

16

The Shannons and Wally rode horseback beside the buggy holding Gwen, Matt, and Lindy, all dressed in their best finery. It was a rowdy, happy bunch that went to the church. Pastor Ingram and his wife were available and eager to facilitate the marriage.

Gwen stood before the preacher, her hand in Matt's, Lindy at her side. Matt's brothers and Wally crowded around them.

Joy overflowed Gwen's heart. To be part of such a large, loving unit amazed her.

The preacher spoke the words uniting Gwen and Matt in marriage. They signed the documents making it legal.

"Lindy can ride with me," Luke offered.

"Wait. I have something for her," Gwen called. She pulled the doll she'd finished from her satchel. "Lindy,

I made this for you. You can play with it anywhere you want. I wanted you to have it to celebrate this special occasion. I hope you like it."

Lindy hugged the doll to her neck. "I love her. I'm going to call her...." She considered her answer. "Birdie."

Luke lifted her to his saddle. Lindy held the doll in front of her, smiling widely. Waving, the men rode away. Matt lifted Gwen to the buggy and climbed up beside her.

"Shall we go home, Mrs. Shannon?"

"I couldn't think of anywhere I'd sooner be."

He waited until they had left town before he stopped and kissed her. "I must be the happiest man on earth."

"And I, the happiest woman." They resumed the journey. "Matt, I never thought I'd have this."

He quirked an eyebrow at her. "What do you mean?"

She lowered her gaze. She wanted Matt to understand her doubts and fears. "I never thought a man would value me. Just for me." She was saying it poorly, but she knew his love wasn't dependent on what she did. He loved her for who she was.

He pulled the wagon to a halt. "Why not? The way I see it, a dozen men must be back east, mourning the fact that they didn't ask you to marry them before you left."

She looked into his dear, kind face. "I never felt loveable before."

"Before now?"

"Yes. To know I'm loved is the greatest feeling." She leaned in and kissed him. She'd meant it to be quick. But he caught her shoulders and pulled her closer for a deep, lasting, promising kiss.

They continued homeward, his arm across her back, her head pressed to him.

"While we're confessing things," he began.

Her heart didn't so much as lurch because whatever he said, it would not be something to hurt her.

"I never felt this way about Corine. I was a young man with a young man's dreams. I didn't know the power of love to heal hurts, to warm my heart, and to promise a future of shared joys."

She wrapped her arms around his waist and squeezed hard. "God has richly blessed us. I am so grateful."

The others greeted them as they returned home. Andy said Lindy would stay in his house for the night. She and Matt hugged the child who said she wanted to show Birdie her old house.

His brothers shook Matt's hand and hugged Gwen and one by one departed.

Luke was the last to say goodbye. "You know, seeing Matt so happy makes me think I should write to that lady friend of yours and ask her to find me a mail-order bride. Someone like you."

"That sounds like a good idea." Gwen waited until Luke left to ask Matt, "Do you think he's serious?"

"I can't say."

He closed the door behind Luke, pulled Gwen into his arms, and kissed her soundly.

"Welcome home, my dear Gwen."

She hugged him hard. A home, a child, and a husband who loved her. God had indeed blessed her beyond her wildest dream.

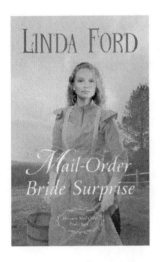

Love challenged.

Truth revealed.

A home where she is welcome.

That's all Honor Ward wants. Oh, and maybe tenderness and yes, even love. She's willing to do most anything to get it...even appear as a mail order bride under false pretenses. She instantly falls in love with her new groom and is determined to prove she is the best wife and homemaker Luke could want. But will her dishonesty make love impossible? How long can she continue her deception?

Seeing how well his twin brother's mail order bride arrangement has turned out, Luke sets out to get himself a woman just like Matt's wife. Honor seems ideal but to his surprise and shock, he learns that Honor is not what she pretends to be. Is this surprise bride exactly what he needs?

Can their fledgling love survive the challenges ahead for them?

ALSO BY LINDA FORD

A heart warming 10 book series where you will meet four Shannon brothers on their ranch in western Montana plus men who worked for them. You will laugh and cry at the situations these men found themselves in when the woman they brought west to marry didn't quite turn out the way they expected. Begin the romantic journey with the first in this series.

Mail Order Mommy

A special collection of stories celebrating 25 years of Linda's writing. It incudes the first book that she ever published, a 2-in-1 novella, and two never published before books that were buried deep in the archives of Linda's computer. Prepare for the tug at your heartstrings with the first in this series.

The Sun Still Shines

This heartfelt series follows three spunky women confronting the wild frontier. The first book in the series tells the story of Glory, the middle sister. She meets a man named Levi, who has devoted his life to preaching God's word. In exchange, he expects God to bring his outlaw brother back into the fold. It sounded easy enough when he made the vow but living it out is proving more difficult than he imagined... especially when he encounters the britches-wearing, horse-riding Glory—the most unusual woman he's ever met.

Glory believes there isn't a man alive who can be trusted.

And that includes the man who claims to be a preacher but looks more like an outlaw. He confuses her, and it isn't long before her heart is involved.

Is Glory just a test for Levi's faith? Or is he the one man she can trust?

Glory and the Raw Hide Preacher

Linda has published over 100 books! Find more available books at https://lindaford.org/books.php

DEAR READER

Thank you for reading Mail-Order Bride Mommy.

I often choose books based on reviews. If you liked this book or have comments would you please go to Amazon and leave a review so others can find it?

If you've enjoyed this story, and would like to read more of Linda's books, you can learn more about upcoming releases by **signing up for her newsletter** at lindaford.org! You will also be able to download a **free** book, *Cowboy to the Rescue*!

Blessings,

Linda Ford

You can also connect with Linda online at:

COPYRIGHT

Made in United States
Troutdale, OR
11/11/2024